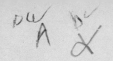

Praise for Kate Hoffmann from
RT Book Reviews

"Sexy and wildly romantic."
—on *Doing Ireland!*

"Fully developed characters and perfect pacing
make this story feel completely right."
—on *Your Bed or Mine?*

"A very hot story mixes with great characters to
make every page a delight."
—on *The Mighty Quinns: Ian*

"Romantic, sexy and heartwarming."
—on *Who Needs Mistletoe?*

"Sexy, heartwarming and romantic…a story to
settle down with and enjoy—and then re-read."
—on *The Mighty Quinns: Teague*

Dear Reader,

The Charmer marks my sixtieth title for Harlequin Books. It's difficult to believe I've reached that milestone. It seems like just yesterday I was sending off my first manuscript and hoping that a publisher might be interested!

I've loved writing stories for Harlequin readers and I hope to continue to do so for many years to come. I've been lucky to find a home here, first with the Temptation line and now with the Blaze line, and you've helped by watching and waiting for my stories—especially for the Quinns.

I also owe a special thanks to my ever-patient editor, Brenda Chin, who has been with me through most of these books and always helps me give you a story that you'll enjoy.

So, this book is for you, the readers. Thank you for all your support over the years, for your letters and e-mails, and for the opportunity to do work that I love so much. There are two more books coming, *The Drifter* in April and *The Sexy Devil* in June, making this another trilogy.

Happy reading!

Kate Hoffmann

Kate Hoffmann

THE CHARMER

TORONTO • NEW YORK • LONDON
AMSTERDAM • PARIS • SYDNEY • HAMBURG
STOCKHOLM • ATHENS • TOKYO • MILAN • MADRID
PRAGUE • WARSAW • BUDAPEST • AUCKLAND

Recycling programs
for this product may
not exist in your area.

ISBN-13: 978-0-373-79524-6

THE CHARMER

www.eHarlequin.com

Printed in U.S.A.

ABOUT THE AUTHOR

Kate Hoffmann has been writing for Harlequin Books since 1993. She's published sixty titles, most with the Temptation and Blaze imprints. Kate lives in southeastern Wisconsin with her cats, Tally and Chloe, and her trusty computer. When she's not writing, she works with local high school students in music and drama activities. She enjoys talking to her sister on the phone, reading *Vanity Fair* magazine, eating Thai food and traveling to Chicago to see Broadway musicals.

Books by Kate Hoffmann

For all my readers, everywhere!

Prologue

Angela@SmoothOperators.com
January 6, 5:30 a.m.
Heading out for my 7:00 a.m. interview on
Daybreak Chicago. Hope you all remember to
tune in. I'm a bit nervous, but excited at the same
time. Call in with questions! I'll post more later.

ANGELA WEATHERBY GLANCED up at her image in the
video monitors, squinting into the bright television
lights that illuminated the studio. She looked worried.
Quickly, she pasted a cheery smile on her face.

The chance to make an appearance on *Daybreak
Chicago* had seemed like a good idea when it had first
been offered. But now, faced with the prospect of airing
her dirty romantic laundry, Angie wasn't so sure.

With her Web site, SmoothOperators.com, she could
be anonymous, just another jilted lover with a score to
settle. But on morning television, for all of Chicago to
see, she might come off looking like a first-class bitch,
out for revenge.

She glanced over at Celia Peralto, her Web master and best friend, who stood next to one of the cameramen. Ceci grinned and gave her a thumbs-up.

A sound technician approached her from behind and clipped a microphone to her collar. "Just tuck the wire under your hair," he advised, "and set the pack on the chair next to you." With trembling fingers, Angie did as she was told.

"Thirty seconds," the producer called.

"Just relax," the host said as she took her place in the opposite chair. "This isn't the Spanish Inquisition. Just a fun segment on single life in Chicago. And it's great publicity for your Web site—and for the book you're planning to write."

The book. Her publisher was expecting the manuscript in three months and though she had gathered all sorts of anecdotal research from her Web site, the book still had to be written.

"Good morning, Chicago! I'm Kelly Caulfield and I'm here with our next guest. About two years ago, Angela Weatherby founded a Web site called Smooth-Operators.com and it has become a national sensation. What began as a way for single girls in Chicago to network over their dating horror stories has evolved into something akin to the FBI's most-wanted list for naughty men."

"I wouldn't put it that way," Angela said. "These men aren't criminals."

"I suspect some Chicago bachelorettes would disagree. Through the Web site, women are helping each other avoid those men who make dating miserable for all of us. And the trend is spreading—the site adds new cities every week. So, tell us, Angela, what gave you the idea for your Web site?"

Angie shifted in her chair, then drew a deep breath. If she just focused on answering the questions, her nerves would eventually calm. "After a series of not-so-nice boyfriends, I felt there had to be a way for me to avoid guys who weren't interested in an honest and committed relationship. I started blogging about it and before long I had over a thousand subscribers. They added their stories and my friend and Web master, Celia Peralto, put their comments into a database. Now, you can check out your date before you even step out the front door. As of last night, we have files on almost fifty thousand smooth operators in cities all over the country."

"Don't you think this is unfair to the men out there? An ex-girlfriend might not be the most objective person to provide commentary."

"You'd check out the plumber you wanted to hire or the doctor you planned to visit, right? We offer information and leave it to our visitors to decide the truth in what they read. And I think we're doing a service. We've even unmasked a number of cheating husbands."

Kelly leaned forward in her chair. "Well, I looked up my cohost, Danny Devlin, and he wasn't very well reviewed on your site. Your rating system goes from one to five broken hearts, with five being the worst. And he's rated a four. Care to comment?"

Angela opened her mouth to reply, then snapped it shut. A glib answer here might turn the interview in a different direction. "Mr. Devlin is always welcome to defend himself. We're open to differing opinions. We just require that the discourse be civilized."

Kelly flipped to her next note card. "Well, that leads us to the book you're writing. Tell us about that."

Angela drew a deep breath and focused her thoughts. She'd practiced her pitch more than once in the mirror at home. "I hope the book will be a guide to the different species of smooth operators out there. Most of these men fall into one of ten or twelve categories. If women can learn to spot them quickly, maybe they'll save themselves a bit of heartbreak."

"And what professional credentials do you bring to the table?" Kelly asked.

"I have an undergraduate degree in psychology, a masters in journalism and experience as a freelance writer. And I've dated a lot of very smooth operators myself," Angie replied, allowing herself a smile. "I'm curious as to why they behave the way they do, as are most women."

"Let's take a few questions from callers," Kelly said. For the next three minutes, Angie jousted with a belligerent bachelor, commiserated with two women who'd just been dumped and fended off the evil glares of Danny Devlin, who had wandered back onto the set. When the six-minute segment was finally over, she sat back in her chair and breathed a sigh of relief.

"You were wonderful!" Kelly exclaimed, hopping out of her chair. "We'll have to have you back again."

"The switchboard went crazy," the producer said as she walked onto the set. "The most calls we've ever had in this time slot. Let's book another interview for next month. Maybe we can do a longer feature segment when the book comes out."

Angie stood up and unclipped the microphone. "That would be lovely," she murmured as she handed it to the sound technician. "Thank you. Is there anything else I need to do?"

"Get that book written," Kelly said. "And personally, I think Danny Devlin deserves five broken hearts. He dumped me by e-mail."

Angie crossed the studio to Ceci, then grabbed her arm and pulled her along toward the exit. "Let's get out of here," she said, tugging her coat on. "Before Danny Devlin corners me and demands that I take his profile off the site."

The early morning air was frigid and the pavement slippery as they walked through the parking lot. When they reached the relative safety of Ceci's car, Angie sat back in the seat and drew a long, deep breath. It clouded in front of her face as she slowly released it. "So, how was I? Tell me the truth. Did I come across as angry or bitter?"

"No, not at all," Ceci said. "You were funny. And sweet. And just a little vulnerable, which was good. You were likeable."

"I didn't seem judgmental? I want people to look at

the Web site as a practical dating tool. Not some orga-
nization promoting hatred of the opposite sex." She
glanced over at Ceci. "I really do like men. I just don't
like how they treat women sometimes."

Ceci smiled as she started the car. "Sweetie, if we
didn't like men so much, we wouldn't waste our energy
trying to fix them. Someone has to hold these guys ac-
countable."

"Did you get through to Alex Stamos?" Angela
asked, turning her attention to the next bit of research
for her book. "He's been ducking my calls for a week
now."

"I got his assistant. She says he's out of town for the
next few days on business, but he'll be sure to get back
to me when he returns. She also mentioned that she had
a few stories of her own about the guy."

"You made it clear that this interview would be
anonymous, didn't you?" Angie asked.

"I said that you wanted to give him a chance to set
the record straight," Ceci said. "But I think getting an
in-depth profile of each of these types might be kind of
tricky. Especially once they've seen the site."

"Maybe I shouldn't do the interviews and go with
my original plan."

"Absolutely not," Celia cried. "I think having a conversation with each of these types makes them real. Just
move on to the next guy on your list and catch up with
Stamos later."

Angie had been working as a freelance writer ever
since she got out of college. It had been a hit-and-miss

career and there were times when she barely had enough to pay the rent. The blog had just been a way to exercise her writing muscles every day, but once it took off, she was able to attract advertisers and make a reasonably constant paycheck from the Web site.

She sighed. Her parents, both college professors, had wanted her to become a psychologist, but when she finished her undergrad studies at Northwestern, she'd decided to rebel and try journalism.

This book would give her instant credibility as a journalist—and it might appease her parents as well as open a lot of doors. The advance alone was nearly gone, lost to car repairs and computer upgrades. Right now, every Tom, Dick and Mary was a blogger. But not many people could say they were a real author.

"You're right," she said. "I can work on Charlie Templeton. Or Max Morgan." But would they be willing to talk? She'd have to readjust her strategy. If the men weren't going to be identified in the book, then maybe a bit of subterfuge to get their stories wouldn't be entirely out of line.

1

ALEX STAMOS PEERED into the darkness, the BMW's headlights nearly useless in the swirling snow. He could barely make out the edge of the road, the drifts causing the car to fishtail even at fifteen miles per hour.

He'd done a lot of things to boost business at Stamos Publishing and as the new CEO, that was his job. But until now, he'd never had to risk life and limb to get what he wanted. His cell phone rang and he reached over to pick it up off the passenger seat. "I'm in the middle of a blizzard," he said. "Make it quick."

"What are doing in a blizzard?" Tess asked. "I thought you were leaving for Mexico tonight."

He had decided to put off his midwinter vacation for a few days. Business was much more important than a week of sun and windsurfing at his family's oceanside condo. "I have to take care of this business first. I'm leaving the day after tomorrow."

"Where are you?"

"The middle of nowhere," he said. "Door County."

"Isn't that in Wisconsin?"

"And you failed geography, little sister. How is that possible?"

Tess groaned. "That was in eighth grade."

"There's a new artist I need to see. He hasn't been returning my calls, so I decided to drive up and pay a personal visit."

"Well, I thought you'd want to know. *The Devil's Own* got a great review in *Publisher's Preview*," Tess said. "And the distributors have been calling all afternoon to increase their orders. At this rate, we're going to have to go back for the second printing before the first is out the door, so I just wanted to let you know that I'm going to put it on the schedule for later next week."

Tess was head of production at Stamos Publishing. She and Alex had been working together on his new business plan for nearly a year and this was the first sign that it was about to pay off. Until last year, Stamos Publishing had been known for it's snooze-inducing catalog of technical books, covering everything from lawnmower repair to vegan cookery to dog grooming. But as the newly appointed chief executive officer, Alex was determined to move the company into the twenty-first century. And that move began with a flashy new imprint for graphic novels.

From the time he was a kid, walking through the pressroom with his grandfather, he'd been fascinated by the family business. While most of his peers were enjoying their summers off, he'd worked in the bindery and the production offices, learning Stamos Publishing from top to bottom.

His dream had been to make Stamos Publishing the premier printer in the comic book industry. That way, he could get all the free comic books he wanted. But as he got older, Alex began to take the business more seriously. He saw the weaknesses in his father's management plan and in the company's spot in the market and vowed to make some changes if he ever got the chance.

The chance came at the expense of his family, when his father died suddenly four years ago. His grandfather had come back to run the business, but only until Alex was ready to take over. Now, nearly all the extended Stamos family, siblings, cousins, aunts and uncles, depended upon him to keep the business in the black.

"I'm going to run forty thousand," Tess said. "I know that's double the first run, but I think our sell-through will be good."

"I guess we were right about the graphic novels," he said, keeping his concentration on the road. Though they weren't comic books, they were the next best thing. The edgier stories and innovative art had made them popular with readers of all ages. And Stamos was posed to grab a nice chunk of the market. "What else?"

"Mom is upset," Tess said. "One of her bridge club ladies showed her that Web site. The cool operators site."

"Smooth operators," he corrected. "What did she say?"

"That a nice Greek boy won't find a nice Greek wife if he acts like a *malakas*. And she also said the next time you come to Sunday dinner, she's going to have a conversation with you."

"Great," Alex muttered. A conversation was always

much more painful than a talk or a chat with his mother. No doubt he'd be forced to endure a few blind dates with eligible Greek girls, handpicked by the Stamos matriarch.

"Some people think that any P.R. is good P.R. I don't happen to agree, Alex. I think you need to do some damage control and you need to do it fast. I'm looking at your profile on this page right now and it's not good. These women hate you. Heck, I hate you, and I'm your sister."

"What do you suggest? I'm not about to talk about my love life in public."

"Who suggested that?"

Alex cursed beneath his breath. "The owner of the Web site called to interview me. Angela…I can't remember her last name. Weatherall or Weathervane."

"She wants to talk to you?"

"I guess. Either that, or she wants to yell at me. But I'm almost certain I've never dated her." He cursed softly. "What makes her think I'm the one at fault here? Some of these women are just as much to blame. They were ready to get married after three dates."

"You have had a lot of girlfriends. Listen, Alex, I know you're a nice guy. So why can't you find a nice woman?"

The car skidded and he brought it back under control, cursing beneath his breath. "I'll figure this out when I get back."

"So this artist must be pretty good for you to drive through a blizzard to see him."

"A little snow is not going to stop me," he replied.

"And this guy isn't just good, he's…amazing. And oddly uninterested in publication. The novel came through the slush pile and I figure the reason he's avoiding me is because he's got another publisher interested."

"So, you're just going to drive five hours in the snow and expect he'll want to talk business?"

"I'm a persuasive guy," Alex said. "My charm doesn't just work on the opposite sex. Besides, if I'm his first offer, then I have a chance to get a brand-new talent for a bargain-basement price. I'm not leaving without a signed contract."

The car skidded again and Alex dropped his phone as he gripped the wheel with two hands. He gently applied the brakes and slowed to a crawl as he fished around for the BlackBerry. But he couldn't find it in the dark. "I have to go," he shouted, "or I'll end up in the ditch. I'll call you after I check in."

"Let me know when you're settled," Tess replied.

Alex found the BlackBerry and tucked it in his jacket pocket, then turned his attention back to the road. He knew Door County was well populated, at least in the summer. But in the middle of a Wisconsin winter, the highway was almost desolate between the small towns, marked only by snow-plastered signs looming in the darkness.

Was he the only one crazy enough to be out during a blizzard? Alex leaned forward, searching for the edge of the road through the blowing snow. A moment later, he realized he was no longer in control of his car.

Without a sound the car hit a huge drift and came to a silent stop in the ditch.

This time, Alex strung enough curse words together to form a complete sentence, replete with plenty of vivid adjectives. He wasn't sure what to do. The car wouldn't go forward or backward. Even if he got the car back on the road, it was becoming impossible to see where the road was. He didn't have a shovel, so there wasn't much chance of getting himself out of the ditch.

Alex grabbed his gloves from the seat beside him and pulled them on. If he could clear some of the snow from beneath the wheels, he might be able to get back on the road. If not, he'd call the auto club for a tow. He grabbed a flashlight from the glove box, then crawled out of the car, his feet sinking into a three-foot drift.

Even with the flashlight, it was impossible to see through the blowing snow. Blackness surrounded him as he dug at the snow with his hands. But for every handful of snow he pulled away, two more fell back beneath the tire. Alex knew the only safe option was to wait in the car for help.

He pulled out his phone to call for a tow, but his gloves were wet and his fingers numb from digging in the snow. The BlackBerry slipped out of his fingers and disappeared into the snowdrift. "Shit," he muttered. "From one bone-headed move to the next." Was it even worth searching for the phone?

He decided against it, figuring the BlackBerry would be ruined anyway. As he struggled back to the door, headlights appeared on the road. For a moment, he wondered if the car would even see him in the blinding snow, but to his relief, the SUV stopped. He waded through the drift as the passenger-side window opened.

"Hi," he called, leaning inside. "I'm stuck."

A female voice replied. "I can see that."

Alex could barely make out her features. She wore a huge fur hat with earflaps and a scarf wound around her neck, obscuring the lower part of her face. In truth, she was bundled from top to toe, except for her eyes. "Can you give me a ride into town?"

"No," she said. "I've just come from town. The road is nearly impassable. I'm on my way home."

Her voice was soft and kind of husky…sexy. He felt an odd reaction, considering it was the only thing that marked her as a woman. "I'd call for a tow, but I lost my cell phone."

"Get in," she said. "I'll take you to my place and you can call from there."

"Let me just get my things from the car." By the time Alex retrieved his duffel, his laptop and his briefcase from the BMW, he was completely caked with snow. He crawled into the warm Jeep and pulled the door shut. "Thanks," he said. He glanced over his shoulder to find two dogs in the backseat, watching him silently, their noses twitching. The larger of the two looked like a lab mix and the smaller had a fair bit of terrier in him.

"What are you doing out on a night like tonight?" she asked.

"I could ask the same of you," Alex said with a grin. "I'm glad you were as brave as I was."

"Stupid is more like it. And I'm not driving a sports car," she said.

"It's not a sports car," he said. "It's a sedan." He glanced over at her. It was impossible to tell how old she was. And the only clue to her appearance was a lock of dark hair that had escaped from under her hat. "Do you live nearby?"

"Just down the road."

He settled back into the seat, staring out at the swirl of white in front of them. He couldn't see the road at all, but she seemed to know exactly where she was going, expertly navigating through the drifts. Before long, she slowed and turned off the highway onto what he assumed was a side road and then a few minutes later, into a narrow driveway, marked by two tall posts, studded with red reflectors. The woods were thick on either side, so it was easy to find the way through the trees.

A yard light was visible as they approached and, before long, Alex could see the outline of a small cabin made of rough-hewn logs. She pulled up in front and turned to face him. "The front door's unlocked," she said. "I'm just going to put the Jeep in the shed."

Alex grabbed his things from the floor and hopped out, then walked through another knee-deep drift to get to the front steps. As he stamped the snow off his ruined loafers, the dogs joined him, racing through the darkness to the porch.

He opened the door a crack and the animals pushed their way into the dimly lit interior. The cabin was one huge room, with a timbered ceiling and tongue and groove paneling. A stone fireplace covered one wall and windows lined the other. The décor was like nothing he'd ever seen before, every available space taken with bits and pieces of nature—a bird's nest, a basket of acorns, a single maple leaf in a frame on a bent-willow table.

He kicked off his shoes and stepped off the rug, but then froze as the dogs growled softly. They'd seemed so friendly in the car, but now they watched him suspiciously as he ventured uninvited into their territory.

"The phone is over there."

He turned to see her standing in the shadows on the other side of the kitchen. "Do they bite?" he asked.

"Only if I tell them to," she murmured. There was a subtle warning in her tone. It wasn't surprising, considering she just allowed a stranger into her home. For all she knew, he could be some deranged psycho— driving an expensive European sedan and wearing ruined Italian loafers.

"I won't make any sudden moves," he said.

She shrugged and walked out of the room, her heavy boots leaving puddles of water on the floor. Alex slipped out of his coat and tossed it over a nearby chair, then kicked off his shoes. When the two dogs approached, he held his breath. They sniffed at his feet, then each picked up a shoe and retreated back to the sofa with their prizes.

"Give those back," he pleaded. "No, don't do that. You can't eat those." Alex heard footsteps behind him and he spun around, coming face-to-face with a woman of peculiar beauty. He glanced around the room. "Hello," he said.

He slowly took in the details of her face. She wore dark makeup on her eyes and her shoulder-length hair was cut in a jagged way, with streaks of purple in the bangs. Was this the woman who had rescued him? He'd imagined the face that went with the voice, speculated about the body, but this wasn't at all what he'd expected.

"They eat shoes," she said, grabbing the loafers and handing them back to him.

Only when he heard her voice was Alex certain. This *was* the woman who had rescued him. But the instant attraction he felt was rather disconcerting. She was the exact opposite of women he usually pursued. He liked blondes, tall and willowy, surgically enhanced and trainer-toned. This girl was petite, with an almost boyish figure, and a quirky sense of fashion.

"Put them in the closet," she said, pointing to a spot near one door. "They don't know how to operate a doorknob…yet. They're still working on tearing strangers limb from limb."

Alex smiled, but she didn't return the gesture. She continued to regard him with a cool yet slightly wary stare. After he'd dropped his shoes in the closet, he surveyed his surroundings. "Nice place. Do you live here alone?"

"No," she said. "There are the dogs. And two cats. And I have two horses down in the barn."

"A regular Noah's Ark," he teased. She gave him an

odd look and he decided be more direct. "So, you're not married?"

"Are you?"

"No," he said, chuckling. Crossing the room, he held out his hand. "I'm Alex Stamos." He waited, growing impatient with the long silence between them. "Now, you're supposed to tell me your name."

"Tenley," she said, refusing his gesture.

"Is that your first or last name? Or both. Like Ten Lee?"

She shook her head. "I haven't had dinner yet. Are you hungry?"

"I could eat, Tenley," Alex said. Odd girl with an odd name. Yet, he found her fascinating. She didn't seem to be interested in impressing him. In truth, she didn't seem the least bit fazed by his charm.

Strange, Alex thought to himself. Women usually found him utterly mesmerizing from the get-go. He slipped out of his jacket and draped it over a nearby chair. His pants were damp and his socks soaked through.

"You should probably call for a tow. Or your car is going to get covered by the drifts. The phone is over there."

"I'll call the auto club." He paused. "I don't have the phone number. It's on my BlackBerry, which is in the snowbank."

"I'll call Jesse. He has the garage in town." She walked over to the phone and dialed. Alex watched her from across the room, studying her features. She really was quite pretty in an unconventional way. Alex drew a slow breath. She had a really nice mouth, her lips full and lush.

When she turned to face him, he blinked, startled out of a brief fantasy about the body beneath the layers of winter clothes. "He won't be able to get to you for a while," she said. "Maybe not until the morning."

"Did you tell him that wasn't acceptable?"

This caused a tiny smile to twitch at the corners of her mouth—the first he'd managed. "No. He's busy. There are more important people than you stuck in the snow. You're safe and out of the storm. Your car can wait. Now, if it's acceptable to you, I'll make us something to eat."

Alex cursed beneath his breath. He hadn't gotten off to a very good start with Tenley. And hell, spending the evening in her company, sharing an intimate dinner, was far more intriguing that sitting alone in his room at the local bed-and-breakfast. "Can I give you a hand?" he asked, following her to the kitchen.

HE SAT ON A STOOL at the kitchen island, his elbows resting on the granite counter top, his gaze following her every move. The tension between them was palpable, the attraction crackling like an electric current.

What had ever possessed her to bring this man in from the storm? She thought she was doing a good deed. He probably would have survived just fine on his own. She could have come home, called the sheriff and let law enforcement ride to the rescue. But now it looked like she'd be stuck with him for the rest of the night.

Tenley was accustomed to a solitary existence, just her, the dogs, the cats, the horses and those occasional demons that haunted her dreams. Having a stranger in the house upset the delicate balance—especially a stranger she found so disturbingly attractive.

In truth, she wasn't sure how to handle company. Since the accident almost ten years before, she'd made a habit of isolating herself, always maintaining a safe distance from anything that resembled a relationship. It was just easier. Losing her brother had sapped every last bit of emotion out of her soul that she didn't have the energy or the willpower to engage in polite conversation. And that was what people expected in social situations.

"Stop staring at me." Tenley carefully chopped the carrot, focusing on the task and trying to ignore Alex's intent gaze. She felt her face grow warm and she fought the urge to run outside into the storm to cool off.

There was work to do in the barn; the horses had to be fed. She didn't have to stay. But for the first time in a very long time, Tenley found herself…interested. She wasn't sure what it was, but his curious stare had her heart beating a bit quicker and her nerves on edge. From the moment he'd offered his hand in introduction, she'd felt it.

Maybe it was just an overreaction to simple loneliness. She had been particularly moody this winter, almost restless. In years past, she'd been happy to hide out, to take long walks in the woods, to spend time with her animals, indulging in an occasional short-lived affair. But this winter had been different. There had been no men and the solitude had begun to wear on her.

She handed him a carrot to munch on, using the opportunity to study him more closely. Alex Stamos. For some reason, the name sounded familiar to her, but she couldn't put her finger on why. He was here on business. Maybe he was one of those real estate developers from Illinois, interested in building yet another resort on the peninsula. She'd probably seen his name in the local paper.

And she didn't understand this sudden attraction. Tenley was usually drawn to men who were a little rougher around the edges, a bit more dangerous. She usually chose tourists who were certain to leave at some point, but she had indulged with a number of willing single men from some of the nearby towns. Her grandfather called them "discardable," and Tenley had to agree with his assessment.

Tenley looked down at her vegetables. There weren't many women who'd kick Alex Stamos out of their bed.

Tenley glanced up again, to find him still staring. She drew a deep breath and met his gaze, refusing to flinch. For a long time, neither one of them blinked.

"I like this game," he said. "My sister and I used to play it when we were kids. I always won."

"It makes me uncomfortable," Tenley said. "Didn't anyone ever tell you it wasn't polite to stare?"

He shrugged and looked away. "Yeah, but I didn't

think that applied in this case. I mean, it's not like you have a big wart on the end of your nose or you've got two heads. I'm staring because I think you're pretty. What's wrong with that?"

"I'm not pretty," she muttered. She grabbed an onion and tossed it at him, then shoved the cutting board and knife across the counter. "Here, cut that up."

She didn't invite this attraction. In fact, over the past year, she'd done her level best to avoid men. The last man she'd invited into her bed hadn't been just a one-night stand. She'd actually found herself wanting more, searching for something that she couldn't put a name to.

She knew the risks. Physical attraction led to sex which led to more sex which led to affection which ultimately led to love. Only love didn't last. It was there one day and gone the next. She'd loved her brother, more than anyone else in the world. And when he'd been taken from her, she wasn't sure she'd ever recover. She wasn't about to go through that again.

"I'm wondering why you wear all that makeup. I mean, you don't need it. I think you'd look prettier without it."

"Maybe I don't want to look pretty," Tenley murmured.

Alex chuckled at her reply. "Why wouldn't you want to look pretty? Especially if you are?"

The question made Tenley uneasy. She didn't tolerate curious men, men who wanted to get inside her head before they got into her bed. What business was it of his why she did what she did? He was a complete stranger and didn't know anything about her life. Why bother to act as if he cared?

She turned and tossed the chopped carrots into the cast-iron pot on the stove. Maybe the town's speculation about her would come true. She'd slowly devolve into an eccentric old spinster, living alone in the woods with only her animals to talk to.

"Do you like peppers?" she asked, turning to open the refrigerator.

"Do you ever answer a direct question?"

"Red or green? I prefer red."

"You don't answer questions," Alex said. "Red."

Tenley gave him a smile. "Me, too. They're sweeter." She handed him the pepper, then grabbed a towel from the ring beneath the sink. Bending over the basin, she quickly washed the makeup off her face, wiping away the dark liner and lipstick with dish soap.

When she opened her eyes again, she found an odd expression on his face. "Better?"

"Yeah," he said softly, his gaze slowly taking in her features. "You just look…different." He paused. "Beautiful."

She swallowed hard, trying to keep herself from smiling. "Thank you," she murmured. "You're beautiful, too."

The moment the words were out of her mouth, she wanted to take them back. This was what came from spending so much time alone, talking to herself. She expressed her thoughts out loud without even realizing it.

He opened his mouth, then snapped it shut. "Thanks."

"I'm not just saying that. You are. Objectively, you're very attractive." Oh, God, now she was just digging a deeper hole. "I just noticed, that's all. I'm not trying to…you know."

"I don't know," he said. He picked up the pepper and walked around the island to the sink, then rinsed it off. "But you could try to explain it to me."

There was no going back now. "The way you're looking at me. I just get the feeling that you're…flirting."

He turned and leaned back against the edge of the counter. "I am. Is there something wrong with that?"

"It's not going to work. I—I'm not interested in…that."

"What?"

"Sex," she said.

He frowned, then shook his head. "Is that what you think I'm doing? I was just having some fun. Talking. I didn't mean to—"

"I didn't want you to think that I was—"

"Oh, I didn't. I guess, I'm just used to—"

"I understand and I don't mean to—"

"I do understand," he said softly. He took a step toward her and she held her breath.

This was crazy. She wanted him to kiss her. With any other man, she would have already been halfway to the bedroom. But Alex was different. All these strange feelings stirred inside of her. She longed for his touch, yet she knew how dangerous it would be. Need mixed with fear and she wasn't sure what to do.

But then Alex took the decision out of her hands. He smoothed his hand over her cheek and bent closer. An instant later, his lips met hers and Tenley felt a tremor race through her body. He lingered over her mouth, taking his time, waiting for her to surrender.

With a soft sigh, Tenley opened beneath the gentle assault. A delicious rush of warmth washed through her body. Lately, she hadn't felt much like a woman. It was amazing what one kiss could do to change all that.

She pushed up on her toes, eager to lose herself in the taste of him. It didn't matter that they'd just met. It didn't matter that she knew nothing about him. He made her feel all warm and tingly inside. That was all she cared about.

He drew back slightly, his breath warm against her mouth. "Maybe we should get back to dinner," he suggested.

With a satisfied smile, Tenley stepped out of his embrace. They did have the entire night. With the blizzard raging outside, there was no way he'd be able to get into town. "There's white wine and beer in the fridge and red wine in the cabinet above. Pick what you want."

"What are you making?" He stood over her shoulder and peered into the cast-iron pot steaming on the stove. "It smells good."

"Camp supper," she said. "It's just whatever's at hand, tossed into a pot. There's hamburger, potatoes, peppers, carrots and onions. I think I'll add some corn."

It wasn't gourmet. Cooking had never been one of her talents. In truth, Tenley wasn't really sure what she was good at. Right about the time she was ready to find out, her life had been turned upside down. Her grandfather was an artist and so was her father. And her mother was a poet, so creativity did run in her veins.

But like everything else in her world, she'd been too afraid to invest any passion in her future for fear that it might slip through her fingers. So she chose to help her grandfather further his career by running his art gallery. At least she knew she was good at that, even though it was more of a job than a passion.

Alex retrieved a bottle of red wine from the cabinet and set it on the counter. She handed him a corkscrew and he deftly dispatched the cork and poured two glasses of Merlot. "This is a nice place," he said.

"It belonged to my grandparents. My great-grandfather built it for them as a wedding gift. After my grandmother died, my grandfather moved into town, and I moved here."

"What do you do?"

"I was just going to ask you the same thing," Tenley said, deflecting his question. "What brings you to Door County in the middle of a blizzard? It must be something very important."

"Business," he replied. "I'm here to see an artist. T. J. Marshall. Do you know him?"

Tenley's breath caught in her throat and for a moment she couldn't breathe. This man had come to see her grandfather? How was that possible? She was in charge of her grandfather's appointments and she didn't remember making one for— Oh, God. That was where she knew his name. He'd left a string of messages on her grandfather's voice mail. Something about publishing a novel. Her grandfather already worked with a publisher and he didn't write novels, so she'd ignored the messages. "I do. Everyone knows him. What do you want with him?"

"He sent us a graphic novel. I want to publish it."

Tenley frowned. Her grandfather painted landscapes. He didn't even know what a graphic novel was. She, however, did know. In fact, she'd made one for Josh Barton, the neighbor boy, as a Christmas gift, a thank-you for caring for her animals. "Do you have it with you?" she asked, trying to keep her voice indifferent.

"I do."

"Could I see it?"

"Sure. Do you like graphic novels?"

"I've read a few," she replied.

"This one is incredible. Very dark. The guy who wrote this has got some real demons haunting him. Or he's got a great imagination. It's about a girl named Cyd who can bring people back from the dead."

Alex walked across the room to fetch his briefcase. Tenley grabbed her glass of wine and took three quick gulps. If this was her work, how had it possibly gotten into Alex's hands? Perhaps Josh had decided to start a career as an artist's agent at age fourteen?

Alex returned with a file folder, holding it out to her. "The story is loaded with conflict and it's really edgy. It's hard to find graphic novels that combine great art with a solid story. And this has both."

Tenley opened the folder and immediately recognized the cover of Josh's Christmas gift. She sighed softly as she flipped through the photocopy. What had he done? He'd raved about the story, but she'd never expected him to send a copy to a publisher. It had been a private little gift between the two of them, that was all. Josh had shared his love of the genre with her and she'd made him a story of his very own. She'd never intended it for public consumption.

Tenley had always had a love-hate affair with her artistic abilities. Though establishing her own career in art might make sense to the casual observer, Tenley fought against it. She and her brother had always talked about striking out on their own, leaving Door County and finding work in a big city. She'd wanted to be an actress and Tommy had been interested in architecture.

But after the boating accident, Tenley had given up on dreams. Her parents had been devastated and their grief led to a divorce. There was a fight over where Tenley would live and in the end, they let her stay in Door County with her grandparents while they escaped to opposite coasts.

They still encouraged her to paint or sculpt or do anything worthy with her art. But putting herself out there, for everyone to see, made her feel more vulnerable than she already did. There were too many ways to get hurt, and so many expectations that could never be met. And now, the one time in years that she'd put pen to paper had brought this man to her door. What were the odds?

"This is interesting," she murmured. "But I think someone is messing with you. T. J. Marshall paints landscapes. This isn't his work."

"You know his work?"

"Yes. Everyone does. He has a gallery in town. You must be looking for another T. J. Marshall."

"How many are there in Sawyer Bay?" he asked.

Two, Tenley thought to herself. Thomas James and Tenley Jacinda. "Only one," she lied.

"And you know him. So you can introduce me. Tell me about him. How old is he? What's his background? Has he done commercial illustration in the past?"

What was she supposed to say? That Tenley Jacinda Marshall was the T. J. Marshall he was looking for? That she was twenty-six years old, had never formally studied art or design, and had spent her entire life in Door County? And that she'd never intended anyone, outside of Josh Barton, to see her story?

"I know this will sell. It's exactly what the market is looking for," Alex continued. "A female protagonist, a story filled with moral dilemmas and great pictures."

Was he really interested in paying her for the story? It would be nice to have some extra cash. Horse feed and vet care didn't come cheap. And though her grandfather paid her well, she never felt as if she did enough to earn her salary. Still, with money came responsibility. She liked her life exactly the way it was—uncomplicated.

"I think I'll make a salad," she said.

He reached out and grabbed her arm, stopping her

escape. "Promise you'll introduce me," Alex pleaded, catching her chin with his finger and turning her gaze to his. "This is important."

"All right," Tenley said. "I will. But not tonight."

He laughed. "No, not tonight." He bent close and dropped a quick kiss on her lips, then frowned. "Are you ever going to tell me anything about yourself?"

"I don't lead a very exciting life," Tenley murmured, as he smoothed his finger along her jaw. A shiver skittered down her spine. His touch was so addictive. She barely knew him, yet she craved physical contact. He'd come here to see her, but somehow she knew that revealing her identity would be a mistake—at least for the next twelve hours.

"You rescued me from disaster," he said. "I could have frozen out there."

"Someone would have come along sooner or later," she said.

They continued preparations for dinner in relative silence. But the thoughts racing through Tenley's mind were anything but quiet. In the past, it had always been so simple to take what she wanted from a man. Physical pleasure was just a natural need, or so she told herself. And though she chose carefully when it came to the men who shared her bed, she'd never hesitated when she found a suitable sexual partner.

This was different. There was an attraction here she'd never felt before, a connection that went beyond the surface. He was incredibly handsome, with his dark hair and eyes, and a body that promised to be close to perfection once he removed his clothes. He was quite intelligent and witty. And he seemed perfectly capable of seducing her on his own.

It might be nice to be the seduced rather than the seducer, Tenley thought. But would he move fast enough? They only had this one night. Sometime tomorrow, he'd find out she was the artist also known as T. J. Marshall. And then everything would change.

"Would you like some more wine?" Alex asked.

Tenley nodded. "Sure." The bottle was already half-empty. Where would they be when it was gone?

THEY HAD DINNER in front of the fire. The sexual tension between them wasn't lost on Alex. By all accounts, the setting was impossibly romantic—a blazing fire, a snowstorm outside and the entire night ahead of them. With any other woman, he could have turned on the charm and had her within an hour. But there was something about Tenley that made him bide his time. She wasn't just any woman and she seemed to see right through him.

In the twelve years he'd been actively pursing women, Alex had honed his techniques. He'd found that most women were turned off by a man who wanted jump into bed after just a few hours together. Though he usually felt the urge, he'd learned to control his desires. He never slept with a woman on the first date. Or the second. But by the third, there were no rules left to follow.

Now he was finding it difficult putting thoughts of

seduction out of his head. He wasn't sure he was reading the signs correctly. Though he found Tenley incredibly sexy, he wasn't sure they were moving in that direction. One moment she seemed interested and the next, she acted as though she couldn't care less.

Though the conversation between them was easy, it wasn't terribly informative. He'd learned that Tenley had lived in Door County her entire life and that the cabin had belonged to her grandparents. Her father was an artist and her mother, a poet. Though she didn't say for certain, he gleaned from her comments that they were divorced. When he asked where they lived, she'd quickly changed the subject.

She kept the conversation firmly focused on him, asking about his business, about his life in Chicago, about his childhood. She seemed particularly interested in the market for graphic novels and his interest in publishing them.

"My grandfather started the company in 1962," Alex explained. "He used to do technical manuals, then started a line of how-to books, right about the time everyone was getting into home improvement. He retired and my father expanded our list to include other how-to titles. *How to Groom a Poodle, How to Make a Soufflé, How to Play the Ukulele.* Real page-turners."

"And then you came along with an idea for graphic novels."

"I've read comic books since I was a kid. But they're not just comic books anymore. They're an incredible mix of graphic art and story. They've turned some of the best ones into movies, so they're starting to move into mainstream culture."

"And this book by T. J. Marshall? Why do you like it?"

"It's…tragic. There's this heroine who, after a brush with death, discovers she can bring people back to life. But she's forced to choose between those she can save and those not worthy. The power only works for a short time before it's gone again. And there's this governmental agency that's after her. They want to use her powers for evil."

"And you liked her—I mean, *his* art?"

"Yeah," Alex replied. "The drawings have an energy about them, a rawness that matches the dark emotion in the story. I find it pretty amazing that someone could be such a great writer and an incredible artist, too."

"So you just want to publish it? Just like that?"

Alex shook his head. "No. There are some things that need to be addressed. The story needs to be expanded. There's a subplot that has to be fleshed out. I've got minor questions about the character, some inconsistencies in the backstory. And we'd want to explore a story arc for a sequel or two, maybe make it a trilogy."

She frowned. "A trilogy?"

"Yeah. We'd want to publish more than one novel. The real success in publishing is not in buying a book, but in building a career."

"So it pays a lot of money?"

"Not a lot. It would depend on how the books sold. But we have a great marketing department. I think they'd do really well. Well enough to provide a comfortable living for the artist."

Tenley quickly stood and gathered up the remains of their dinner. He got to his feet and helped her, following her into the kitchen with the empty bottle of wine. Though he hadn't quite figured out her mercurial mood changes, he was finding them less troublesome. She just moved more quickly from one thing to the next than the ordinary person, as if she became bored or distracted easily.

"Can I help you with the dishes?" he asked, standing beside her at the sink.

"Sure," she murmured.

He reached across her for the soap, his hand brushing hers. The contact was startling in its effect on his body. A current raced up his arm, jolting him like an electric shock. Intrigued, he reached down and took her hand in his, smoothing his fingers over her palm.

"You have beautiful hands," he said, examining her fingers. It was as if he knew these hands, knew exactly how they'd feel on his face, on his body. Her nails were painted a dark purple and she wore several rings on her fingers and thumb.

Alex slowly pulled them off, setting them down on the edge of the sink. It was like undressing her in a way, discovering the woman beneath all the accoutrements. He drew her hand up to his lips and placed a kiss on the back of her wrist.

Her gaze fixed on his face, her eyes wide, filled with indecision. Alex held his breath, waiting for a reaction.

He kissed a fingertip, then drew it across his lower lip. The gesture had the desired effect. She leaned into him and a moment later, their mouths met.

Unlike the experiment that was their first kiss, this was slow and delicious. She tasted sweet, like the wine they'd drunk. He pulled her close, smoothing his hands over her back until her body was pressed against his. Kissing her left him breathless, his heart slamming in his chest.

He ran his hands over her arms, then grasped her wrists and wrapped them around his neck. A tiny sigh slipped from her throat and she softened in his embrace, as if the kiss were affecting her as much as it was him.

Alex had made the same move with any number of women, but it had never had this kind of effect on him. What was usually carefully controlled need was now raw and urgent. He wanted to possess her, to get inside her soul and find out who this woman was. She was sweet and complicated and vulnerable and tough. And everything about her drew him in and made him want more.

Maybe that was it. He'd learned well how to read women, to play on their desires and to make them want him. But Tenley was a challenge. She didn't react to his charm in the usual ways. Yet that wasn't all he found so intriguing. She lived all alone in the woods, with a bunch of animals. Where was her family? Where were the people who cared about her? And how did a woman as beautiful as Tenley not have a boyfriend or a husband to take care of her?

He sensed there was something not right here, something he couldn't explain. Alex felt an overwhelming need to reveal those parts of her that she was trying so hard to hide. She'd rescued him out on the road, but now he suspected that she was the one who needed saving.

The diversion was short-lived. The phone rang and, startled by the sound, Tenley stepped back. Her cheeks were flushed and her lips damp. "I—I should get that."

Alex nodded as she slipped from his embrace. She hurried to the phone and picked it up, watching him from beneath dark lashes. He leaned back against the edge of the counter and waited, certain they'd begin again just as soon as the call was over. But when she hung up, she maintained her distance.

"Jesse towed your car into town," she said.

"Good."

"But not before the snowplow hit it. He says it's not real bad. It'll need a new back bumper and a side panel. And a taillight. And a few more things."

Alex groaned. "Can I still drive it?"

"No. I don't think so."

"Great," he muttered. "How the hell am I going to get around?"

"I guess I'll have to drive you," Tenley said. "You're not going to be going anywhere tonight anyway, so it's not worth worrying about. Jesse says the wind is just blowing the roads closed right after they plow them." She crossed back to him. "I—I should go out and check on the horses."

"I'll come with you," Alex suggested.

"It's late. You're probably tired. You can have the

guest room. It's at the end of the hall. There are towels in the closet outside the bathroom. Just help yourself."

With that, she fetched her boots from a spot near the back door, then pulled on her jacket. A moment later, she stepped out into the storm. Alex opened the door behind her and watched as she disappeared into the darkness. The cold wind whipped a swirl of snow into his face and he quickly closed the door and leaned back against it.

What had begun as a simple business trip had taken a rather interesting turn. But he wasn't sure whether he ought to take his chances and hike into town, or spend the night under the same roof as this utterly captivating and perplexing woman.

He grabbed his duffel and walked to the guest room. When he finally found the light switch, he was surprised to find two cats curled up on the bed. The two calicos were sleeping so closely, he couldn't tell where one ended and the other began. Neither one of them stirred as he dropped the bag on the floor. But when the dogs came bounding into the room, they opened their eyes and watched the pair with wary gazes.

"Time to go," he said, picking them each up and gently setting them on the floor. They ran out the door, the dogs following after them.

Alex shut the door, then flopped down on the bed. He closed his eyes and let his thoughts drift back to the kiss he'd shared with Tenley. Though he hadn't had any expectations of further intimacies, he wished they hadn't been interrupted. With each step forward, he found himself curious about the next.

Though he'd enjoyed physical pleasure with lots of women, this was different. Everything felt…new. As if he were experiencing it for the first time. He groaned softly. He wanted her, in his arms and in his bed. But wanting her was as far as he would go. He was a guest in her house and wasn't about to take advantage, no matter how intense his need.

He'd come here to do a job, to sign T. J. Marshall to a publishing contract. It wouldn't do to get distracted from his purpose.

2

THE WATER WAS SO COLD and black. Even with her eyes open, she couldn't see her hand in front of her face. *Stay awake, stay awake.* A voice inside her head kept repeating the refrain. Or was it Tommy? Was he saying the words?

Her nails clawed at the fitting on the hull of the boat as it bobbed in the water. *Stay with the boat. Don't try to swim for shore.* Though she wore a life jacket, Tenley knew that sooner or later her body temperature would drop so low it wouldn't matter. She wouldn't drown. She'd just quietly go to sleep and drift out into the lake.

"Tommy!" She called his name and then felt his hand on hers. "I'm sorry. I'm sorry." She grasped at his fingers, but they weren't there. He wasn't there. He'd decided to swim for it, ordering her to stay with the boat. "I'll be back for you," he called. "I promise."

How long had it been? Minutes? Hours? Tenley couldn't remember. Why was she so confused? She called his name again. And then again. Over and over until her voice was weak and her throat raw.

The sound came out of nowhere, a low rumble, like

the engine of a boat. It was Tommy. He'd come, just as he'd promised. But as the roar came closer, Tenley realized it wasn't a boat at all but a huge wave, so high that it blocked out the moon and the stars in the sky. She held her breath, waiting for it to crash down on top of her. Where had it come from?·

A ton of water enveloped her, driving her deep beneath the surface. The breath burned in her lungs and she struggled to reach the cold night air. Maybe it was better to let go, to stop fighting. Was that what Tommy had done? Was he safe at home, or had the black wave taken him as well? No, she wouldn't. She couldn't. She—

Tenley awoke with a start, sitting upright in her bed, gasping for breath. For a moment, she wasn't sure where she was. She rubbed her arms, only to find them warm and clad in the soft fabric of her T-shirt. She was safe. But where was Tommy? Why wasn't he—

A sick feeling settled in her stomach as she realized, yet again, that Tommy was gone. There were times when she had such pleasant dreams about their childhood. They'd been the best of friends, twins, so much alike. As the only children of a poet and an artist, they'd grown up without boundaries, encouraged to discover all that nature had to offer.

Back then, they'd lived on the waterfront, in the apartment above her grandfather's studio. The sailboat had been a present from her grandfather for their thirteenth birthday and every summer, she and Tommy had skimmed across the harbor, the wind filling the small sail and the sun shining down on them both.

But as they got older, they became much more daring. Their adventures had an edge of danger to them. Diving from the cliffs above the water. Wandering into the woods late at night. Sailing beyond the quiet confines of the harbor to the small islands just offshore.

They'd both known how quickly the weather could shift in the bay and how dangerous it was to be in a small boat when the waves kicked up. But they both loved pushing their limits, daring each other to try something even more outrageous.

A shiver skittered through her body and Tenley pulled the quilt up over her arms. It had been her idea to sail out to the island and spend the night. Even though the wind had been blowing directly into shore and they'd gotten a late start, they'd tacked out, the small Sunfish skimming over the bay at a sharp angle.

But sailing against the wind had taken longer than she'd anticipated and by the time they'd reached open water, it was nearly dark. Tommy had insisted that they head back toward the lights, but Tenley had been adamant, daring him to go on. A few minutes later, a gust of wind knocked the boat over.

It was usually easy to right the boat in the calm waters of the harbor, but in the bay the currents worked against them, exhausting them both. Tenley could see the outline of the island and suggested they swim for it. But in the dark, it had been impossible to judge how far it was. In the end, Tommy had left to get help.

They'd found her clinging to the boat, four hours later. They'd found his body the next morning, washed up on a rocky beach north of town. Tenley shook her head, trying to rid herself of the memories. It had been nearly a month since she'd last dreamt of him. In many ways, she'd longed for the nights when the dreams wouldn't haunt her. But sometimes, the dreams were good. They were happy and she could be with her brother again.

She threw the covers off her body and stood up beside the bed, stretching her arms over her head. The room was chilly, the winter wind finding its way inside through all the tiny cracks and crevices in the old cabin. Outside, the storm still raged.

Tenley rubbed her eyes, then wandered out of the bedroom toward the kitchen. She rarely slept more than four or five hours at night. For a long time, she'd been afraid to sleep, afraid of the nightmares. But she'd learned to cope, taking the good dreams with the bad.

The dogs were curled up in front of Alex's door and they looked up as she passed. Tenley stirred the embers of the fire and tossed another log onto the grate. As she watched the flames lick at the dry birch bark, her mind wandered back to the kiss she'd shared with Alex in the kitchen.

She'd been tempted to let it go on, to see how far he'd take it. The attraction between them was undeniable. But she wasn't sure she wanted to act upon it. She preferred uncomplicated sex and Tenley sensed that sex with Alex might be like opening a Pandora's box of pleasure.

Restless, she got up and began to pace the perimeter

of the room. She had no idea what time it was. Tenley had given up clocks long ago, preferring to let her body decide when it was time to sleep and when it was time to wake up. Besides, since Tommy's death, she'd never slept through an entire night so what was the point of a schedule?

Tenley grabbed a throw from the back of the leather sofa and wrapped it around her, then slowly walked down the hall to the guest-room door. Dog and Pup were still asleep on the floor, pulling guard duty, defending her safety. Perhaps the dogs knew better than she did about the dangers that lay beyond the door.

"Up," she whispered, snapping her fingers softly. They both rose, stretched, then trotted off to her bedroom. Holding her breath, Tenley opened the door and peeked inside.

Alex's face was softly illuminated by the bedside lamp and Tenley crossed the room to stand beside the bed. His limbs were twisted in the old quilt, a bare leg and arm exposed to the chilly air in the room. Tenley let her gaze drift down from his handsome face and tousled hair, to the smooth expanse of his chest and the rippled muscles of his belly.

An ache deep inside her took her breath away and she felt an overwhelming need for physical contact, anything to make her feel again. She'd pushed aside her emotions for so long that the only way to access them was to lose herself in pleasure. Until now, all she really required was a man who wouldn't ask for anything more than sex. But now, watching Alex sleep, she yearned for a deeper connection, a way back from the dark place where she'd lived for so long.

Was he the light she was looking for? Tenley rubbed her eyes with her fingers. Then reaching out, she held her hand close to his skin, surprised at the heat he generated. If she were warm and safe, she could forget the dream, forget the guilt. All she needed was just a few minutes of human contact.

A shiver skittered through her and without considering the consequences, she lay down beside him, tucking her backside into the curve of his body. Tenley felt him stir behind her and she closed her eyes, waiting to see what might happen.

He pushed up on his elbow and gently smoothed his hand along her arm. She glanced over her shoulder to find a confused expression on his face. Slowly, she rolled onto her back, their gazes still locked. Then, Tenley slipped her hand around his nape and gently pulled him closer, until their lips touched.

The kiss sent a slow surge of warmth through her body as he gently explored her mouth with his tongue, teasing and testing until she opened fully to his assault. With a low moan, he pulled her body beneath his. They fit perfectly against each other and Tenley arched into him, desperate to feel more.

The memories of the nightmare slowly gave way to a tantalizing pleasure. Alex ran his hand along her leg and beneath the T-shirt, then stopped suddenly, as if surprised that she wore nothing beneath. Giving him permission to continue, she slipped her fingers beneath the waistband of his boxers, searching for an intimate spot to explore.

But as the touching grew more intense, the clothing they wore seemed to get in the way. Frantic to feel his naked body against hers, Tenley sat up and tugged her T-shirt over her head, then tossed it aside. She heard his breath catch and she smiled. "It feels better without clothes."

He grinned, then skimmed his boxers off, revealing the extent of his arousal. Unafraid to take what she wanted, Tenley wrapped her fingers around his hard shaft and gently began to stroke him. The caress brought a moan from deep in his throat and his fingers tangled in her hair as he drew her into another long, deep kiss.

"Am I awake or am I dreaming?" he asked, his lips soft against hers, his voice ragged.

"You're dreaming," she whispered.

"It doesn't feel like a dream," he countered. He cupped her breast with his palm and ran his thumb over her nipple. "You're warm and soft. I can hear you and taste you."

"Close your eyes," Tenley said. "And don't open them until I get back."

She crawled off the bed, but he grabbed her hand to stop her retreat. "Don't leave."

"I'll be right back. I promise. Close your eyes."

He did as he was told and Tenley hurried out of the room to the bathroom. She rummaged through the cabinet above the sink until she found the box of condoms, then pulled out a string of plastic packets.

When she returned to the room, he was sitting up in bed, waiting for her. She held up the condoms. "I think we might need these."

He chuckled. "All of those?"

Tenley felt a blush of embarrassment. It had been a while since she'd had a man in her bed. Once might not be enough. "Yes," she said. "All of them."

"I think you might be overestimating my abilities," he teased.

"And you might be underestimating mine," she replied.

When she got close to the bed, he grabbed her hand and yanked her on top of him. "Tell me what you want. I'll do my best to comply."

She wanted to lose herself in the act, to let her mind drift and her body take flight. She wanted to forget the past and the present and future and just exist in a haze of pleasure. She wanted the warmth and touch of another human being. And most of all, she wanted that wonderful, exhilarating feeling of release with a man moving deep inside her.

She tore a packet off the strip and opened it, then, with deliberate care, smoothed it down over his erection. Without any hesitation, Tenley straddled his hips and lowered herself on top of him. When he was buried to the hilt, she sighed. "This is what I want," she murmured, her eyes closed, her pulse racing.

"Me, too," he whispered.

ALEX HADN'T BEEN prepared for how good it would feel. Maybe because it had all been so unexpected.

He'd always taken his time charming a woman, knowing that once he got her to bed, his interest would soon wane. But from the moment Tenley had lain down beside him, Alex knew something remarkable was about to happen.

This wasn't some game he was playing, a diversion that he found interesting until something better came along. This was pure, raw desire, stripped of all artifice and expectations. He closed his eyes and sighed, reveling in the feel of her warmth surrounding him.

He didn't care what it meant or where it would go after this. All he knew was that he wanted to possess her, even it if was just for an hour or two on a snowy January night.

His fingers tangled in her hair and he drew her to his mouth. Though she didn't possess any of the attributes he normally found attractive in a woman, he couldn't seem to get enough of her. Her skin was pale, but incredibly soft. And her breasts, though small, were perfect. She was everything he'd never had before—and never wanted. Alex smoothed his hands over her chest and down her torso to her hips. Then he sat up, wrapping her legs around his waist and burying his face in the curve of her neck.

Tenley moved against him, her head tipped forward and her eyes closed. Her hair fell across her face and he reached up and brushed it aside, watching as desire suffused her features. Though he wanted to surrender to his own passion, Alex found it far more fascinating to watch her.

The intensity of her expression made him wonder what was going through her mind. She seemed lost in her need, searching for release in an almost desperate way. He reached down between them and touched her. A soft cry slipped from her lips and Alex knew he could give her what she wanted.

Her breath came in deep gasps and he focused on the sound, trying to delay the inevitable. And then, she was there, dissolving into spasms, her body driving down once more, burying him deep inside her.

It was all Alex could take, watching her orgasm overwhelm her. He surrendered to the sensations racing through his body and a moment later, found his own release.

Tenley nestled up against him, her arms draped around his neck, her lips pressed to his ear. "Oh, that was nice," she whispered.

"Umm," he replied, too numb to put together a coherent sentence. "Very nice."

She drew back, a wicked smile curling her lips. "You want to do it again?"

"No, not quite yet," he said with a chuckle. "Just let me catch my breath for a second." Alex wrapped his hands around her waist and pulled her down beside him, dragging her leg up over his hip. "This is a nice way to spend a snowy night." She shivered and Alex rubbed her arm. "Are you cold?"

Tenley shook her head. "Would you like some hot chocolate? I feel like some." She crawled out of bed and walked to the door, naked. "Are you coming? It makes a really good nightcap."

With a groan, Alex rolled out of bed. First, incredible

sex and then hot cocoa. He didn't know much about her, but she was a study in contradictions. Grabbing the quilt off the bed, Alex wrapped it around himself and followed her to the kitchen.

The room was dark, lit only by the flames flickering in the fireplace. She opened the refrigerator and he stood and stared at her body, so perfect in the harsh white light. "You are beautiful," he said.

"No," Tenley replied. "You don't have to say things like that to me. I don't need reassurance. I wanted that as much as you did."

"I'm just telling you what I think," Alex said. "You don't take compliments well, do you?"

"No," she said. "They make me…uncomfortable."

"Personally, I love compliments," he teased.

She poured milk into a pan and set it on the stove. The burner flamed blue and she turned it to a low simmer. "I think you have nice eyes," she said. "And I like your mouth."

"Thank you," he replied. "I like your mouth, too."

"Thank you," she said.

"See, that wasn't so bad."

"The key to making good hot chocolate is in the chocolate. You have to use real cocoa and sugar, not those powdered mixes."

He sat down on a stool and wrapped the quilt more tightly around him. "I was always of the opinion that marshmallows were the key. You can't use the small ones. You have to use the big ones. They melt slower."

Tenley opened a cabinet above the stove and pulled

out a bag of jumbo marshmallows, then tossed them at him. "I totally agree. Bigger is better."

"Oh, another compliment. Thank you."

She giggled. "You're welcome." Tenley turned back to the stove and Alex got up and circled around the island to stand behind her. He wrapped the quilt around her, pulling her body back against his. Just watching her move had made him hard again.

She tipped her head as he pressed his lips to her neck. "Why do you smell so good? What is that?"

"Soap?" she said. "Shampoo."

"I like it." The women he'd known had always smelled like a perfume counter. But Tenley smelled clean and fresh. He closed his eyes and drew a deep breath, trying to commit the scent to memory. "I'm glad you came into my room," he whispered.

She turned to face him, then pushed up on her toes and gently touched her lips to his. "It's too cold to sleep alone." Tenley brushed his hair out of his eyes and smiled. "Cocoa. I need cocoa."

After she'd retrieved a container from a nearby cabinet, Tenley measured out the cocoa and stirred it into the milk, before adding a generous handful of sugar. Then she picked up the pan and poured the steaming drinks into two huge mugs that were nearly full of marshmallows.

"Let's sit by the fire," she said, grabbing the mugs.

Alex followed her, spreading the quilt out on the floor in front of the hearth. She seemed just as comfortable naked as she did clothed, stretching out on her stomach and offering him a tempting view of her backside.

"What are you doing here?" he asked.

She took a sip of her hot chocolate, then licked the melted marshmallow from her upper lip. "Relaxing?"

"That's not what I meant. I meant, here, all alone, in this cabin. Why isn't there someone here with you?"

She rolled over and sat up. "Like a roommate?"

"Like a man," he said.

"I like being alone. I don't really need a man." She paused. "Not that I don't enjoy having you here."

The words were simple and without a doubt, the truth. "I can always head back out into the storm, if you'd rather be alone," he offered.

"No. It's nice to have company every now and then."

"Someone to talk to?"

"Someone to touch," she said. Tenley reached out and placed her hand on his chest. "Aren't there times when you crave physical contact?" She paused. "Never mind. I suppose you just go find a woman when that happens, right? Men have it easy. No one questions your need for sex."

"And they question yours?"

"Not they. Me. I guess that comes with being a female. We aren't supposed to want it like men do."

"And do you want it?" Alex asked.

"I'm not afraid to admit that I enjoy it," she said. "Sex makes me feel...alive."

"Good to know," Alex said. He took her mug from her hand and set it down on the floor, then cupped her face in his hands. "You are the strangest girl I've ever met."

"Weird strange?"

"Fascinating strange," he replied.

He gently pushed her back until she lay on the quilt. Tenley stretched her arms over her head, her body arching sinuously beneath his touch. Taking his time, he traced a line from her neck to her belly with his lips.

He knew how to bring a woman to the edge and back again, and he wanted to do that for Tenley. His fingers found the damp spot between her legs. She responded immediately, her body arching, her breath coming in shallow gasps.

And when his mouth found that sensitive spot, she cried out in surprise. But Alex took his time. He'd always been a considerate lover, but sex had been about his pleasure first. It wasn't that way with Tenley. He wanted to make it memorable for her.

After he was gone, Alex needed to know he would be the standard by which other men in her life might be judged. It was silly, but for some strange reason, it made a difference to him. He wanted her to remember what they shared and continue to crave it.

Her fingers slipped through his hair and he felt her losing control. Alex slowed his pace, determined to make her feel something that she'd never experienced before. Her drew her close, tempting her again and again. She whispered his name in a desperate plea to give her what she wanted.

The sound of her voice was enough to arouse him and to Alex's surprise, he found himself dancing near the edge. He shifted, the friction of the quilt causing a delicious frisson of pleasure to race through him. Gathering his resolve, Alex brought her close again. But this time, it was too much for her.

When he drew back, she couldn't help herself. Tenley moaned, her body tense. An instant later, her orgasm consumed her, her body trembling and shuddering. It was enough to drive him over the edge. Startled, Alex joined her.

He rolled over on his back. This was crazy. He felt like a teenager, with nothing more than his imagination and a little friction standing between him and heaven. Throwing his arm over his eyes, he waited for the last of his own spasms to subside.

"That was a surprise," he murmured. Alex rolled to his side and kissed her hip.

"I've never really liked surprises, until now."

Alex knew how she felt. From the moment she'd rescued him from the snowbank, he'd learned to expect the unexpected from Tenley. He closed his eyes and pressed his face into the soft flesh at her waist. Forget the vacation. Spending time with Tenley was all the adventure he needed.

TENLEY OPENED her eyes to the early morning light. An incessant beeping penetrated her hazy mind and she pushed up on her elbow to survey the room.

After making love in front of the fire, they'd wrapped themselves in the quilt and fallen asleep on the floor. She couldn't remember the last time she'd slept so soundly and for such a long stretch of time.

She sat up and glanced over her shoulder at Alex. He

was a beautiful man, tall and lean and finely muscled. And he knew what he was doing in bed—and on the floor, too. A shiver skittered through her as she remembered the passion they'd shared.

She'd never experienced anything quite so powerful. Usually she used sex to forget. But she remembered every little detail of what she'd shared with Alex, from the way his hands felt on her skin to the taste of his mouth to the soft sound of his voice whispering her name. She felt safe with him, as if she didn't need to pretend.

It had taken so much energy to keep her emotions in check and now, she finally felt as if she might be able to let go, to find a bit of enjoyment in life…in Alex. Tenley didn't know what it all meant, but she knew it felt right.

As she studied his features, she wondered about the women he normally dated. A man like Alex Stamos wouldn't lack for female company. There were probably hundreds of women waiting outside his door, hoping to enjoy exactly what she had last night.

The beeping continued and she crawled around him to find his watch lying on the hearth. Tenley picked it up and, squinting in the low light, tried to turn off the alarm. But when she couldn't find the right button, she got to her feet and carried it into the kitchen. With the soft curse, she opened the refrigerator door and put it inside.

This is exactly why she hated clocks. Simple, inanimate objects in control of a person's life! Was there anything more obnoxious? Well, maybe television.

She didn't own one of those either. She preferred a good book. Although, there were times when she wished she could watch a movie or check out the weather station.

Rubbing her arms against the cold, Tenley returned to their makeshift bed, ready to slip back beneath the covers and wake him up slowly. It was so easy to relax around him, to just be herself without any of the baggage that came along with her past. Everyone within a thirty-mile radius of Sawyer Bay knew about her past. She couldn't walk down the streets of town without someone sending her a pitying look.

She knew what they were saying about her. That she'd never recovered from the tragedy. That she deliberately pushed people away because she blamed herself. It was all true. Tenley was acutely aware of what she'd become. But that didn't make it any easier to forget her part in what had happened. Nor did she feel like changing just to make everyone else more comfortable. It was simply easier to keep people at a distance.

Alex was different. For the first time in her adult life, she wanted to get closer. If Tenley had the power, she'd make the storm go on for another week or two so they could be stranded in this cabin a little longer. There would be quiet afternoons, making love in front of the fire. And then never-ending nights, when sleep could come without dreams.

There was a way to keep him close, Tenley mused. If she accepted his proposal to publish her graphic novel then they'd have an excuse to see each other every so often. Maybe he'd make regular trips up to Door County to see her and they could enjoy these sexual encounters three or four times a year.

Tenley smiled to herself. It was the closest she'd ever come to a committed relationship. But in that very same moment, she realized the risk she'd be taking. Cursing softly, she turned away and walked through the cabin to her room.

"Don't be ridiculous," she muttered to herself as she pulled on her clothes. She and Alex Stamos had absolutely nothing in common, beyond her novel and one night of great sex. What made her think he'd even want a relationship?

He probably had his choice of women in Chicago. Why would he choose to carry on with her? It was a prescription for heartbreak, Tenley mused. She'd make the mistake of falling in love with him, living for the times they could be together, and one day, he'd tell her it was over.

She'd learned how to protect herself from that kind of pain and it wouldn't do to forget those lessons now. Alex was a momentary fling, just like all the other men in her life. She could enjoy him for as long as he stayed, but after that, she'd move on.

As for her novel, it would be best to put an end to that right away. Though a little extra money might be nice, she certainly didn't need the pressure to produce another story.

Tenley tiptoed back out into the great room and found her boots and jacket near the back door. The dogs were waiting and, when she was bundled against the cold, she slipped outside, into the low light of dawn. She bent down and gave them both a rough scratch behind the ears. Pup, the larger of the two, gave her a sloppy kiss on the cheek. And Dog pushed his nose beneath her hand, searching for a bit more affection.

"Go," she said, motioning them off the porch. They ran down the steps and into the snow, leaping and chasing and wrestling with each other playfully. The wind was still blowing hard, the snow stinging her face. She tipped her head back and looked into the sky, still gray and ominous.

A memory flashed in her mind and she remembered the sky on the day she and Tommy had set off on their sail. The image was so vivid it was like a photograph. A storm had taken her brother away. And now another storm had brought Alex into her life. The forces of nature were powerful and uncontrollable.

Was that what this was about? Was nature giving her back what she'd lost all those years ago? She drew a deep breath of the cold air. She'd never believed in fate or karma but she couldn't help but wonder why Alex had suddenly appeared in her life. A few minutes one way or the other, a different day or time, and they never would have met at all. Another shiver skittered down her spine and she started off across the yard.

The barn was set fifty yards from the house, a simple wooden structure painted the traditional red. Attached to one corner was a tower that rose nearly three stories off the ground. Her grandfather had built it as a studio, with four walls made of windows to take in the views of the woods and the bay.

Tenley slogged through the snow to the barn door and retrieved a shovel. She cleared off the stairs to the studio, then stepped inside to escape the icy wind. The stairwell was as cold as the weather outside, but when she opened the door to the room at the top of the stairs, it was pleasantly cozy.

Dropping her jacket at the door, she walked to the wall of windows facing the lake. The snow was still coming down so hard, she wasn't able to see more than a hundred yards beyond the barn.

With a soft sigh, she sat down at the huge drawing table in the center of the room. Her grandfather's easels had moved to town with him, but he'd left his drawing table, in hopes she'd find a use for it.

She and her grandfather had always been close. After Tommy's death, he'd been the only one she could stand to be around. And after her grandmother had died, Tenley had taken over the duties of running the business end of the gallery, a job her grandmother had done since their wedding day.

She did most of her business over the phone and, when customers came in the front door, her grandfather usually greeted them. He hated the details of running the gallery and she avoided the customers. It had been a good arrangement. If she weren't working for him, he'd have to hire someone at a much higher salary. All Tenley needed was enough to buy food and clothes and feed for her animals.

She sifted through the sketches scattered over the surface. Her work was a mishmash of genres and media. A pen-and-ink drawing of a hummingbird, a pastel landscape, a watercolor self-portrait. She'd never been to art school, so she'd never really discovered what she was good at.

Grabbing a cup filled with black markers, she sat down at the table. Taking a deep breath, she sketched a scene with her heroine, Cyd. She imagined it as a proper cover for the novel, something that would set the mood for the story inside.

There was a generous portion of Tenley in her character. She was an outsider, a girl who had known tragedy in her life, one who was graced with an incredible power. But with that power came deep moral dilemmas. Tenley often wondered what it would be like to change the past, to alter the course of history.

What would her life be like if she hadn't teased her brother into sailing to the island? Or if the weather hadn't turned on them? What if they'd stayed home or left earlier? Where would she be today?

Tenley closed her eyes and tried to picture it. Would she be married, happily in love with a man, surrounded by their children? Or would she be living in some big city, working as an artist or a writer? She'd always thought about becoming an actress.

Perhaps her parents wouldn't have divorced and maybe her grandmother wouldn't have suffered the stroke that killed her. Maybe the townspeople of Sawyer Bay would admire her, rather than pity her. Snatching up the drawing, Tenley crumpled it into a ball and tossed it to the floor.

She couldn't change the past. And she didn't want to change the future. There was a certain security in knowing what her life was, in the sameness of each passing day. "I'm happy," Tenley said. "So leave well enough alone."

She grabbed her jacket and pulled it on, then headed back down to feed the horses. The dogs joined her in the barn, shaking the snow from their thick coats. As she scooped feed into a bucket, the horses peeked over the tops of their stall doors.

"Sorry, ladies. No riding today. But after breakfast, you can go outside for a bit." The two mares nuzzled her as they searched for a treat—a carrot or an apple. But Tenley had left so quickly she'd forgotten to bring them something. "I'll be out later," she promised.

On her way back to the house, Tenley decided to walk up to the road and see if it had been plowed. The woods kept the snow from drifting too high, but it was clear they'd had at least sixteen or eighteen inches since it began yesterday morning.

By the time she reached the end of the driveway, Tenley could see they'd be stuck in the cabin for another day. A huge pile of snow had been dumped across the driveway and beyond it, the road was a wide expanse of bare pavement and three-foot drifts.

In truth, she was happy to have another day with Alex. If they spent it in the same way they'd spent the night before, then she wouldn't have reason to grow impatient with the weather. Tenley smiled as the dogs fell into step beside her. "We'll keep him another day," she said.

The cabin was quiet when she let herself back in. She stripped off her jacket and boots, then shimmied out of her snow-covered jeans. The dogs were anxious to eat and they tore through the great room in a noisy tangle of legs and tails.

"Ow! What the hell!" Tenley looked up to find Pup lying across Alex's chest, his nose nudging Alex's chin.

"No!" she shouted. "Come here!"

Pup glanced back and forth between the two of them, then decided to follow orders. Alex sat up and wiped his face with the damp quilt. "Funny, I expected someone of an entirely different species to wake me up."

"Sorry. If you want to get some more sleep, you should probably go to your room. Once the dogs are up, they're up."

"What time is it?" He glanced at his wrist. "I lost my watch."

She opened the refrigerator and pulled it out. "It wouldn't stop beeping."

Alex got to his feet and walked naked to the kitchen, then took the watch from her grasp. He strapped it onto his wrist, silencing the alarm. Then, he looked at the clock on the stove and noticed it was almost noon. "Is that right?" he asked, rechecking his watch.

She shook her head, trying to avoid staring at his body. "No. I don't like clocks. There isn't any need for them here."

Alex frowned, raking his hand through his hair. "What about when you have to be somewhere on time?"

"I never have to be anywhere on time. I get there when I get there."

Alex chuckled. "I wish I could live like that," he murmured.

She glanced over her shoulder at him. He was so beautiful, all muscle and hard flesh. Her fingers twitched as she held out her hand. "You could. Here, give me your watch."

"No. This is an expensive watch."

"I was just going to put it back in the refrigerator."

He thought about the notion for a second, then smiled and slipped it off his wrist. "When in Rome."

She opened the fridge and put it inside the butter compartment. "You've been liberated. Doesn't that feel good?"

"How do you know when to get up in the morning?"

"I usually get up when the sun rises," she explained. "Or when the dogs wake me."

"Don't you have to be to work at a certain time?"

She shrugged. "I keep my own hours." She opened a cabinet and pulled out two cans of dog food. "Here, make yourself useful. The can opener is in that drawer."

"I thought I had made myself pretty useful last night," he murmured.

Tenley felt a warm blush creep up her cheeks. "You want to talk about it?" she asked.

"You…surprised me. I wasn't expecting…"

"Neither was I," she said. "I was curious."

"About me?"

She nodded. "Sure. You seemed like you were interested."

"I was," he said. "Am. Present tense. But I'm even more curious about something else."

"What's that?"

"Whether it might happen again?"

A tiny smile curved the corners of her mouth. "Depends upon how long this storm lasts." So it wouldn't be just a one-night stand. Tenley wasn't sure how she felt about that. She wanted to spend more time with him, even though she knew she shouldn't. But she liked Alex. And he lived in Chicago, so sooner or later, he'd head back home.

A brief, but passionate affair, one that wouldn't be dangerous or complicated. As long as she kept it all in perspective. It wouldn't last long enough to become a relationship. And if it didn't become a relationship, then she couldn't possibly get hurt. Still, she had to wonder what he was thinking about it all. Why not just ask? "What if it does happen again," she asked. "And again. What would that mean?"

He gave her an odd look. "It would probably mean we'd have to go out for condoms?" he teased. Alex paused, then shrugged, realizing that she didn't find much humor in his joke. "It would mean that we enjoy each other's company. And that we want to get to know each other better?"

"Then it wouldn't be a relationship?" she asked.

"It could be," he said slowly.

"But if we didn't want it to be?"

Alex drew a deep breath. "It will be whatever you want it to be," he replied. He glanced over his shoulder, clearly uneasy with the turn in the conversation. "Maybe we should check out a weather report so we can plan our day," Alex suggested. "Where's your television?"

That was it, Tenley thought. She knew exactly where he stood and she was satisfied. Neither one of them were ready to plan a future together. Still, if she did ever want a man in her life, someone who stayed more than a few nights, Alex would be the kind of guy she'd look for. "I don't have a television," she said.

He stared at her in astonishment. "You don't own a television? How is that possible? What about sports and the news?"

"There's never a need. I have a radio. They do the weather every hour on the station from Fish Creek. It's over there in the cabinet with the stereo. But you really don't have to check the weather. The storm is going to last for a while."

"How do you know that?"

"The barometer. Over there, by the door. It hasn't started going up yet. When it does, the storm will start to clear."

"Does that mean you can come back to bed?"

"Maybe we should try a real bed?" she suggested. Tenley tugged her sweater over her head and let it drop on the floor. Then she turned and walked toward her bedroom, leaving a trail of clothes behind her. The storm wouldn't last forever, so they'd best put their time to good use.

3

ALEX WASN'T A meteorologist, but from what he could see outside, the storm showed no signs of weakening. Though he had business to attend to, he was content to spend the day with Tenley, sitting in front of a warm fire with a comfortable bed close at hand.

Without his watch, he could only guess at the time, probably early afternoon. But Tenley was right. It didn't matter. He didn't have anywhere important to be. T. J. Marshall could wait.

He rolled onto his side and watched Tenley as she slept. He'd known her for less than a day, yet it seemed as though they'd been together for much longer. In truth, he'd spent more time with her than he had with any single woman over the past ten years. And considering he'd never spent a complete night in a woman's bed, this was another first.

He thought about their earlier discussion. She'd made it very clear she wasn't interested in anything more than a physical relationship. And he'd agreed to her terms. But Alex was already trying to figure out whether there was more between them than just great sex.

He reached out and smoothed a lock of hair from her eyes. She didn't possess the studied perfection of most of the girls he'd dated. Everything about her was much more natural, more subtle. She was…soft and sweet.

Yet she also had an edge to her, an honesty that caught him off guard at times. There wasn't a filter between her thoughts and her mouth, just a direct line. But he was beginning to enjoy that. Though she didn't answer every question he asked, when she did, he could trust that he was getting the truth.

Alex stretched his arms over his head. He needed to call the office or see if he could get an Internet connection. He smiled to himself. She didn't have a television. She probably wouldn't find a home computer particularly useful either.

He slipped out of bed and walked to the bathroom, deciding to grab a shower. He flipped on the water in the shower stall and waited for it to warm up, then looked at his reflection in the mirror. He needed a shave first.

Alex shut off the water, then retrieved his shaving kit from the guest room. After plucking a razor and a can of shaving cream out of the leather case, he rinsed his face off and continued to stare into the mirror. He was exhausted, but it was a pleasant exhaustion, a sated feeling that he hadn't felt in…a long time? Ever. He'd never felt this way after making love with a woman. In truth, intimacy always left him restless.

Alex heard the bathroom door creak behind him and a few seconds later, he felt her hands smooth over his back. She rested her cheek on his shoulder and watched him in the mirror.

"I thought you were asleep," he said. "I was just going to catch a quick shower and shave." He slowly turned and she smiled. "What do you want?"

"Nothing," she said. "What do you want?"

"I need a shave," Alex replied.

She reached around him for the can of shaving cream he'd set on the edge of the sink. "I can help with that." Tenley sprayed some cream on her palm, then patted it onto his face.

"Are you sure you know what you're doing?"

"No," she said. "But I do shave my legs. It can't be much different. Hand me the razor."

Alex grabbed it and held it over his head. "Be careful. We're a long way from emergency medical care. And this pretty face is all I have."

She took the razor from his hand, then stepped closer. "You are full of yourself, aren't you?" Her hips pressed against his and he slipped his arms around her waist to steady them both. Slowly, she dragged the blade over his skin, her brow furrowed in concentration.

Alex held his breath, waiting for disaster, but Tenley took her time. And as she worked at the task, he found himself growing more and more aroused. There was something about her taking on this mundane part of his life, even if it was as simple as shaving, and making it erotically charged.

With a low moan, he moved his hands down to her hips, his shaft growing harder with every second that passed. Was it possible to want her any more than he already did? Every time he thought his need might be sated, he found himself caught up in yet another sexual encounter, more powerful than the last.

"Quit squirming," she warned. "I'm almost finished."

"Finished?" He chuckled, running his hands up to her breasts. "Look what you started."

"It really doesn't take much, does it?" Tenley teased.

"From you, no." Why was that? Alex wondered. Why did every innocent touch seem to send all the blood to his crotch? What kind of magical power did she hold over him?

"You know," she murmured, "we're lucky we're snowed in."

"What do you mean?"

"Because if we have to take care of your little problem every time it pops up, we'd never get out of the house."

"We could always take a shower together and see how that goes. Maybe it will just disappear."

"I know exactly how to get it to disappear," she said. "Come on." Tenley grabbed his hand and pulled him out of the bathroom, bits of shaving cream still on his face. "You'll love this."

They walked through the house, both of them stark naked. Then she opened the coat closet and rummaged around inside until she pulled out a pair of boots. "Here, put these on."

"Oh, wait a minute. Is this going to get kinky? You want me to be the lumberjack and you're going to be the... I don't know, what are you going to be?"

"Just put them on."

"Why?"

"Do it," Tenley said. She grabbed her own boots from the mat beside the back door and tugged them on, then flipped a switch beside the door. A red light blinked. "Ready?" she asked, her hand on the door.

"For what?"

"Just follow me." Tenley yanked the door open, then stepped outside onto the back porch.

Alex gasped. "What the hell are you doing? You're naked. You'll freeze to death."

"Not if I run fast enough," she cried. With that, she scurried across the porch to the steps, then carefully waded through the drifted snow.

If this was Tenley's idea of fun, then Alex was going to have to expose her to more interesting events—concerts, ball games, nightclubs. Drawing a deep breath, he walked through the open door and pulled it shut behind him. She stood waiting, her hair blowing in the wind, her skin pink from the cold.

"You have to move fast, before you start to feel the cold," she cried.

"I already feel it." He glanced down to notice that the erection she'd caused had subsided and the effects of the cold were beginning to set in. "Tenley, come on. I don't want to play in the snow."

"Follow me," she called. She headed toward a small log building. When she turned and waved to him, her foot caught on something beneath the snow and she disappeared into a snowdrift.

With a sharp curse, Alex took off after her. By the time he got there, she'd already picked herself up and was laughing hysterically, snow coating her hair and lashes and melting off her warm body.

"What the hell are you laughing about?"

"I picked a bad time to be a klutz," she said. Tenley grabbed his hand and led him to the tiny log hut, then opened the door. She reached inside and pulled out two buckets. "Here, fill these with snow." She grabbed two for herself and scooped them into a nearby drift.

By this time, Alex could barely feel his fingers, much less the other appendages on his body. But when the buckets were filled, she led him inside the hut. To his surprise, it was warm and cozy inside.

Cedar benches lined three walls and a small electric stove was positioned in the center. "Wow. A sauna."

Tenley set the buckets next to the stove and stretched out on one of the benches. "My grandfather built this for my grandmother. She was Finnish and she grew up with one of these. Her family was from northern Michigan. They didn't have indoor plumbing so this is the way they took a bath. Except they'd cut a hole in the ice afterward and jump in."

"We're not going to do that are we?"

"No, we'll just roll around in the snow. It works the same way."

"And this is what your family does for fun?"

"Yes. What does your family do?"

He chuckled. "We don't roll around naked in the snow. We…eat. And argue. Occasionally, we play board games or watch movies. I grew up with typical suburban parents. My mother would be shocked to hear I was running around without any clothes on."

She smiled. "I was raised a bit differently. My parents were very open-minded. Free thinkers. They taught us that being naked was perfectly natural."

"Hey, I'm all for nudity. In warm weather."

"You'll love it. I promise. It's invigorating. And relaxing." She made a sad face at him. "Don't be such a baby. You city boys don't know what you're missing."

"Believe me, there is no way I'd ever miss this."

Tenley crawled across the bench and stood in front of him. Then she gently pushed him back. "Sit," she said. "Relax. Take a load off."

Alex did as he was told, leaning back against the rough wall of the cabin. Tenley knelt down in front of him, running her hand along the inside of his thighs. "You're very tense," she said.

"It was freakin' cold out there."

"Relax," she said, smoothing her hands over his belly and then back down his legs. Alex watched her as she explored his body, her touch drifting down to his calves. She tugged off the boots and tossed them aside, then massaged his feet.

This was definitely worth the run through the cold, he mused, tipping his head back and closing his eyes. "Those Finns have the right idea," he said.

She pushed his legs apart and knelt between them, pressing her lips to his chest. Alex knew what was coming, but the rush of sensation that washed over him came as a surprise. Her lips and tongue were sweet torture, making him hard and hot in a matter of seconds. He wondered if it might be dangerous to become aroused in such a warm environment, then decided that if he died as a result, he'd go out a happy man.

He'd experienced this same pleasure with other women before, but he'd always focused on his own enjoyment, taking what was offered without thinking much about his partner. But as Alex watched Tenley seduce him with her mouth, he realized that she wasn't just any woman. The pleasure with her was more intense, more meaningful, because she was the one giving it.

He never understood how a guy could be satisfied spending his whole life with just one woman. But he was beginning to see how it was possible. Tenley was like a dangerous drug, alluring and addictive. The more he had of her, the more he needed.

Though he tried to delay, Alex's release came hard and quick. One moment he was in control and the next, he was caught in a vortex of incredibly intense pleasure. When he finally opened his eyes, he found Tenley staring up at him, a satisfied smile on her face.

"I told you saunas could be relaxing," she said.

"I will never doubt anything you say. Ever. Again."

"ARE YOU HUNGRY?" Tenley asked.

Alex distractedly rubbed her stockinged feet as he read, his long legs stretched out in front of him. Tenley sat on the opposite end of the leather sofa, trying to finish *Madame Bovary,* but she found her study of Alex much more intriguing. She'd been focusing on a tiny scar above his lip, wondering how it got there.

"No, I'm fine," he murmured.

They'd returned from the sauna and snow bath, tumbled into bed for another round of lovemaking, then taken a quick shower together. After a long and leisurely breakfast at two in the afternoon, Alex had rebuilt the fire and they'd settled in, listening to the wind rattling the windows and the drifting snow hissing against the glass.

"I should probably go check on the horses," she said. "I was going to let them out for a while."

He glanced up at her. "Don't you ever just sit still? Chill out. Just be with me."

"So, you liked the sauna?" she asked. Though it took every ounce of persuasion to get him out there, Tenley considered the activity a success. Alex, naked, in any environment, was fun.

"It was just about the best thing I've ever experienced," he said, his gaze still fixed on the book he was reading.

"We could play a game," she said. "Do you like Scrabble?"

He snapped the book shut. "Do I have to have sex with you again, to calm you down? Because if that's what it's going to take, I will. Just say the word. I'm willing to make the sacrifice."

Tenley giggled. "I'm just not used to sitting around. I don't read in the middle of the day. I read before bed because it puts me to sleep."

"If I weren't here, what would you be doing?" Alex asked.

"Clearing the driveway. I have a small tractor with a front-end loader. After that, I'd shovel the walk out to the barn. Then I'd probably get the dogs and take a hike out on the road, to see if it was plowed. Or maybe brave the storm and drive into town for some dinner."

"Is the road clear?" Alex asked.

"No."

"Does it make sense to plow the driveway right now?"

"No."

"Why don't we just talk, then. Have a conversation. I'll ask you a question and you answer it. And then you ask me a question and I'll answer it."

Tenley really didn't like the suggestion. After all, there were a few things she was hiding from him. She wasn't quite ready to tell him she was T. J. Marshall. Though it would certainly make for some interesting conversation, it might change everything between them.

She tried to imagine his reaction. He probably wouldn't be thrilled at her deception. He might wonder what other lies she'd told. But he would have to be happy he'd found her and they'd developed a relationship of sorts. He liked her. How could he be angry for long?

She could always test the waters, Tenley thought. Throw a tiny bit of truth out there and see how it went. "I suppose you're anxious to get into town," she ventured. "I mean, since you have business."

"That can wait," Alex said. "There's not much I can do about it in the middle of this storm."

"The snow should quit in a few hours," she said. "The barometer is starting to rise. Then I can dig us out and you can be on your way." She paused, waiting for his response.

"There's no hurry," he said.

"So you'd like to stay another night?"

He squeezed her foot. "If you'll have me. I'm not too much trouble, am I?"

"No," she said. She drew a long breath, steeling herself for what would come next. "You can meet my grandfather tomorrow morning."

His hand froze on her foot and his brow furrowed. "You want me to meet your family?"

"You came here to see T. J. Marshall, didn't you? That's my grandfather."

Alex gasped, his eyes going wide. "Wait a second. Why didn't you tell me that earlier?"

She shrugged. "I didn't think it made a difference. Does it? Make a difference?"

"You're Tenley Marshall?"

"Yes."

He leaned back into the sofa and raked his hand through his hair, shaking his head. "I just don't understand why you wouldn't have said something."

"Because I thought you might be one of those guys who doesn't like to mix business with pleasure? Because I'm the one who rescued you and I found you attractive? Mostly because I wanted to see what you looked like naked and I figured if you knew who I was, you wouldn't take off your clothes."

Alex thought about her explanation for a moment, then sighed. "I guess I understand. Is there anything else you're keeping from me?"

She shook her head. If she didn't say the word *no*, then it wasn't a full-fledged lie, was it? "My grandfather didn't create that book, though. I run his gallery. I know his work. And that's not his."

"I don't get it. Why would someone send it in under his name? It doesn't make sense."

Tenley jumped off the sofa. "I'm going to take care of the driveway before it starts to get dark. If the weather clears we could drive into town and see about your car."

"Are you that anxious to get rid of me?" he asked.

"No," she said. In truth, Tenley wished she could keep him for the rest of the week. Maybe even for the rest of the month. It was nice to have a man around, if only for the good sex. And the sex was really good. "But we don't have much to eat for dinner. The snow isn't going to plow itself. Besides, it will give you a chance to relax and read."

"I'll come with you," he said. "I can help."

"No, you're the guest. I'll be in soon. You can feed the dogs if you like." She hurried over to the kitchen and retrieved two cans of dog food from beneath the sink.

"You never told me their names, either."

"Dog," Tenley said. "And Pup. The little one is Dog and the big one is Pup," she said.

"Unusual names."

She slipped her bare feet into her boots, then tugged on her jacket. "They just wandered in one day and that's what I called them. Once they decided to stay, I didn't see any reason to give them new names since they seemed quite happy with Dog and Pup."

"Do you always take in strays?" he asked.

"I took you in, didn't I?" She sent him a flirtatious glance, hoping that it might smooth over any ruffled feathers. He chuckled. So she hadn't completely messed things up between them. If this revelation didn't upset him, maybe he'd be fine learning that she was the artist behind the graphic novel he wanted.

She zipped her coat up and pulled the hood tight around her face, then grabbed her gloves from her pockets. Sooner or later, he'd discover the whole truth. And after that, she'd have to try to explain her entire life to him. She could barely make sense of it herself.

Her novel meant money to him. And he'd assume she'd want a share of the financial windfall. But Tenley wasn't sure she wanted to turn a silly little scribble into a job. She wasn't a decent artist. People would criticize and she didn't think she'd be able to take that. Hell, there were a million reasons she could give him to go back to Chicago and leave her alone. But there was only one that made any sense to her.

She was starting to imagine a future with him. Not marriage or children, but a relationship, a connection that went beyond what they shared sexually to something resembling affection and trust. She'd already wondered what it might be like to have him present in her life, to speak to him every day on the phone, to see him on weekends…to make plans.

With a soft sigh, she trudged down the hill toward the shed. "I've spent less than twenty-four hours with the man," she muttered to herself. "It's a little early to confuse good sex with a relationship."

But would she even know a relationship if it dropped out of the sky and landed at her feet? She'd never been in love, never wanted to be with anyone for more than a night or two. Maybe after a second night together, she'd want him to go away.

Tenley waded through a huge drift, then grabbed the shed door and slid it open. Her Jeep was inside, still coated with snow from the night before. The small tractor sat beside it. All these thoughts about the future were beginning to drive her a bit crazy.

Maybe it was time to heed the warning signs, to put a little distance between them. If they spent another night together, there was no telling how she'd feel in the morning. She might just fall in love with Alex Stamos. And Tenley knew that was the worst thing she could possibly do to herself.

ALEX PEERED OUT the window, watching as Tenley maneuvered the tractor around the small yard, scooping up snow and dumping it against the trees. He wasn't quite sure how to take her news. Had he known she was T. J. Marshall's granddaughter, he'd have played things a whole lot differently.

Getting the artist under contract was his first priority. Everything else fell to the bottom of his to-do list. Still, even if he'd wanted to, Alex suspected it would have been impossible to resist Tenley's advances. She did crawl into bed with him, so he wasn't completely to blame.

The only way this could go south is if he and Tenley parted on bad terms. Alex cursed beneath his breath. What if she'd already fallen in love with him? If he didn't handle this right, she could sour a deal with her grandfather before it even began.

Alex stepped away from the window and crossed to the fireplace. Holding his hands out to the warmth, he contemplated the possibilities. If he had to choose between Tenley and the book contract, the choice would have to be— His breath caught in his throat.

No, it wasn't that easy. His first instinct wasn't to put business first. He wanted to choose Tenley. The notion startled him. He'd never made a woman the priority in his life. Beyond his sisters and his mother, women were pretty much a temporary distraction. Work always came first.

Alex shook his head. Maybe it was time to start thinking about business. He crossed the room to the phone, then picked it up and dialed the office. When the receptionist answered, he asked for his sister's extension.

"Where have you been?" she asked. "I've been ringing your cell and it kept bouncing through to your voice mail. I've called all the hospitals up there thinking you got into some kind of accident."

"I'm sorry. I lost my cell in a snowbank and I spent the night with the Good Samaritan who rescued me from the ditch. My car got hit by a snowplow and I haven't had a chance to talk to this artist yet. So, I'm going to be here for a while."

"Sounds like you've had a very exciting twenty-four hours," she said.

"You wouldn't believe it," he said. "I need you to overnight another cell phone to me. Send it to the Harbor Inn in Sawyer Bay. Then find a place for me to rent a car. And have them deliver it to the inn. On second thought, rent an SUV. Once I get into town, I'll try to find a wireless network and I'll pick up my mail."

"What's your number at the inn?" Tess asked.

"I'm not there yet. I probably won't be until tomorrow morning."

"Where are you?"

"I'm staying with this…with T. J. Marshall's granddaughter."

"Oh, that's nice," Tess said. "So things are going well?"

"That's debatable," he said. "And a very long story to tell. But, I should be at the inn sometime tomorrow. I'll call you then."

He set the phone down, then picked up his book from the sofa. *Walden* was one of his favorite books and obviously one of Tenley's as well. She had written notes in the margins and he found drawings at the ends of chapters. Frowning, he walked over to the bookshelves that flanked the fireplace.

He'd noticed the eclectic selection of literature and was quite impressed. But the books hadn't been hers originally. Most of them held copyrights from the 1950s and earlier. The library had probably belonged to her grandfather.

He plucked out a copy of *Jane Eyre* and flipped through it, noticing the notes and drawings. If he looked hard enough, he could see hints of the artist who had drawn Cyd. Alex grabbed another book, *The Catcher in the Rye,* and opened it, only to find a drawing of a young girl on the title page.

The parallels were there to see. In the eyes and in the hands. T. J. Marshall had drawn these sketches and he'd drawn the graphic novel. But according to Tenley, her grandfather only painted landscapes. She'd been adamant that the novel wasn't his work.

Something wasn't right. He wasn't getting the whole story, and Tenley was standing in the way. She worked at her grandfather's gallery. Was she afraid that publishing an edgy graphic novel might hurt his reputation as a serious painter? If that was the case, they could publish under a pseudonym.

Alex needed to meet this man and make his proposal. If the roads were clear, then he'd have Tenley take him into town. If not, he'd go tomorrow morning. But he was definitely not sleeping with Tenley tonight. There was every chance that she was deliberately distracting him.

"Definitely not," Alex repeated. He grabbed the copy of Thoreau and sat down on the sofa. But as he tried to pick up where he'd left off, Alex's thoughts kept returning to Tenley. Sleeping in separate rooms seemed like a good plan, but in reality, he'd have a serious problem staying in his room. And if she crawled into bed with him, then all bets were off.

No, he'd have to get back to town tonight. If Tenley wouldn't take him, then he'd call a cab. Perhaps the inn had a shuttle service.

Over the next half hour, Alex tried to focus on reading, but he found himself walking back and forth to the window, peering out at Tenley as she ran the tractor up and down the driveway. He'd never known a woman who could drive a tractor. But then, he wondered if there was anything Tenley couldn't do for herself. She seemed like the kind of woman who didn't need a man.

When she parked the tractor near the shed and started back toward the house, Alex returned to the sofa and opened his book. She burst through the door, brushing snow off her jacket and stamping her feet on the rug.

"Get your things together," she said. "The road is plowed. I'll take you into town." She opened the closet door and pulled out a down jacket. "Wear this. You'll need something warm. And find a hat. It's still windy."

With that, she turned and walked back outside, slamming the door behind her. Alex stared after her. "I guess I will be sleeping alone tonight, after all." He wouldn't have to worry about controlling his desires. Somehow, he'd rather that the decision had been his.

Alex went back to the guest room and gathered his things, then found the pair of boots he'd worn out to the sauna. When he was dressed against the cold, Alex walked out onto the porch, expecting to find Tenley waiting there with her SUV. But the woods were eerily silent.

He hiked down to the shed, calling her name, the sound of his voice echoing through the trees. As he passed the barn, he noticed her inside. She was working with one of her horses.

"I'm ready," he said, dropping his duffel on the ground.

"I'll just be a few minutes."

"Tenley, I don't want you to think that I'm angry with you. I can understand why you might want to protect your grandfather's reputation."

She gave him a perplexed look. "All right," she said. "You have business to do and sleeping with me is probably just a distraction. It's better that you go."

"You're not a distraction," he said, contradicting what he'd been thinking earlier. "I don't regret the time we spent together. Or anything we did. Do you?"

She smiled and shook her head. "No. I liked having sex with you."

He caught her gaze and held it. Was that all it had been to her? Just sex? "Do you want me to stay the night?"

"You don't have to," she said. "The roads are plowed."

"That's not the point," Alex countered. "I'm asking if you want me to stay another night."

"Have you ever taken a sleigh ride?" she asked, striding out of the barn, the horse following her. She handed him the reins. "Hold these."

"What does that have to do with anything?"

Tenley smiled. "Minnie needs exercise and the roads are perfect. They're covered with snow so they're nice and smooth. It'll be fun." She walked to a large sliding door on the side of the barn and pulled it open to reveal a small sleigh. Then she took the reins from his hands and deftly hitched the horse to the sleigh.

"Hop in," she said, leading Minnie toward him. "You can toss your things in the back."

When they were both settled in the sleigh, a thick wool blanket tucked around their legs, Tenley snapped the reins against Minnie's back and the sleigh slid out into the yard. The horse took the hill up to the road without breaking stride and before long, they were skimming over the snowy road at a brisk pace.

The horse's hooves were muffled by the hard-packed snow. Alex drew a deep breath and let it out slowly, listening to the hiss of the runners beneath them. He glanced over at Tenley, the reins twisted in her hands, her gaze fixed intently on the road.

She was amazing. He'd had more new experiences with her in the past twenty-four hours than he had in the past year of his life. How could he ever forget her? And why would he want to? He scanned the features of her face, outlined by the afternoon sun.

It was all so breathtaking—her beauty, the sparkling snow, the blue sky and the crisp silence of the winter evening. She glanced over at him. But this time, she didn't smile. Their gazes locked for a moment and he leaned over and dropped a kiss on her lips. "This is nice."

"My grandfather used to take my brother and me out after snowstorms. We'd bundle up and my mother would make us a thermos of hot cocoa and off we'd go. We'd sing and laugh and my face would get so cold it would hurt. It's one of my favorite childhood memories."

"I can see why. It's fun. Does he live around here?"

"My grandfather lives in town. I told you, he has a gallery—"

"I meant your brother," Alex corrected.

An odd expression crossed her face. Alex wasn't quite sure how to read it. She looked confused and then sad. Tenley shook her head. "No. He died."

Alex was shocked by her reply. He'd come to believe he knew most of the basic facts about Tenley. But what he'd pieced together obviously still had a lot of holes. Very big holes. "I—I'm sorry. I didn't mean to—"

"No, it's all right. Nobody ever mentions him around me. I'm just not used to talking about him." She pasted a bright smile on her face. "People think I'm…fragile. I'm not, you know."

"I can see that," Alex replied. "I don't know a single woman who can drive a sleigh *and* a tractor. Or run naked through the snow."

"People also think I'm crazy," she said. "You'll probably hear a lot of that when you're in town."

He slipped his arm around her and pulled her body against his. "I like crazy." Alex paused. "I'm going to see your grandfather tomorrow. I'm hoping to convince him to let me publish his novel."

"I know," she said.

"And then, after he's signed a contract with me, I'm going to come back out here for another sleigh ride."

They passed the rest of the trip in complete silence. As they drove into town, Alex was struck by the fact that he'd spent an entire day away from what he considered the conveniences of civilization. There were people driving on the streets and lights that seemed a bit too bright and clocks confirming what the sun had already told him— the day was coming to an end. And it was noisy.

He fought the temptation to grab the reins from Tenley and turn the sleigh around. Their time together had been such a nice respite from his real life, much better than a week at his family's beach condo in Mexico.

They wove through the narrow streets of town, snow piled high and nearly obscuring their view of the white clapboard buildings. She pulled the sleigh to a stop. "I don't know where you were planning to stay," she said. "But this is the nicest place in town. Ask Katie for the big room at the top of the stairs. It has a fireplace."

He caught sight of the sign hanging from the porch. "Bayside Bed and Breakfast," he said. "I had a reservation at the Harbor Inn."

"This is better. Katie Vanderhoff makes cinnamon rolls in the morning." She twisted the reins around a ring near her feet, then jumped out of the sleigh.

Alex followed her around to the back, then grabbed his things from the luggage box. "Thanks for everything. For saving me from the storm, for taking me in and feeding me."

"No problem," she said.

This wasn't going to be easy, saying goodbye to her. Alex didn't like the prospect of spending the night alone in bed. Nor did he want this to be the end. "Let's have dinner tomorrow. I'm going to be staying another night and you probably know of a nice place."

She hesitated, then nodded. "Sure. I'll talk to you tomorrow." Tenley turned to walk toward the sleigh, but Alex didn't want her to leave.

He dropped his things onto the snowy sidewalk, then caught up to her and grabbed her hand. He pulled her against him, his mouth coming down on hers, softly at first, then urgently, as if he needed to leave her with something memorable. Alex searched for a clue to her feelings in the softness of her lips and the taste of her tongue.

She surrendered immediately, her arms slipping around his neck. Time stood still and, for a few moments, Alex felt himself relax. She still wanted him, as much as he wanted her. So why the hell were they spending the night apart?

"Stay with me," he said.

"I can't. I have to take Minnie back. And if I stay here, the whole town will know by tomorrow morning. They already spend too much time talking about me." She pushed up on her toes and kissed him again. "I'll see you tomorrow."

With that, she hopped back into the sleigh and grabbed the reins. The horse leaped into a brisk walk when she slapped the reins against the mare's back and

Alex watched as she disappeared around the corner. A sense of loneliness settled in around him.

Suddenly exhausted, Alex picked up his things and walked up to the porch. When he got inside, he rang the bell at the front desk. A moment later, an elderly woman stepped through a door and greeted him.

"I need a place to stay," Alex said. "I'm told that I should ask for the big room at the top of the stairs."

"Have you had friends that have spent time with us?" she asked.

"No. Tenley Marshall suggested this place."

The woman blinked in surprise. "You're a friend of Tenley's?"

"Yes. Is the room available?"

She nodded. "How is Tenley? I haven't seen her recently. She used to work for me when she was a teenager. But that was before all that sadness." She drew a sharp breath and shook her head, then forced a smile. "I'm glad to know she has a friend."

Alex frowned. Though he wasn't one to pry into other people's private affairs, he believed he had a right to know a little more about the woman who had seduced him. "Yes," he said. "I heard about all that. You'd think after all this time—how long has it been?"

"Oh, gosh. Ten years? She was fifteen or sixteen. They were a pair, those two. Joined at the hip from the moment they were born. And you've never seen such beautiful children. That black hair and those pale blue eyes. You'd never recognize her now with all that silly makeup."

"I think she's beautiful," Alex said, feeling the need to defend Tenley.

She blinked in surprise. "Well, that's lovely." A smile slowly suffused her entire face. "Let's get you registered and then I'll show you your room."

Though he was tempted to ask more, Alex decided to bide his time. He didn't want to give the town gossips any more to chat about.

4

TENLEY CAREFULLY maneuvered the sleigh down the narrow streets to the harbor. Before long, the salt trucks would be out and the snow would melt away, making it impossible to use the sled. They could have brought her truck, but Tenley had wanted time to talk to him, to tell him the entire truth.

Unfortunately, she hadn't been able to figure out a way to adequately explain her reasoning. Forced to come up with an alternate plan, she decided to enlist her grandfather's help. But she needed to talk to him before Alex had a chance to introduce himself. She drew to a stop in front of her grandfather's gallery, then tied the reins to the mailbox.

"What kind of gas mileage do you get with that rig?"

Tenley turned to find the town police chief, Harvey Willis, hanging out the window of his cruiser. He waved and she returned the gesture. "Oats and hay," she said. "And an occasional apple."

"Drive safe," he said. "And get that thing back to your place before dark or I'll be giving you a citation. It doesn't have lights on it." He chuckled, then continued up the road from the harbor.

Her grandfather answered the door after only thirty seconds of constant ringing. He carried a paint-stained rag and wiped his fingers as Tenley greeted him.

"You brought the sleigh out. Give me a few minutes and I'll get my jacket."

"No, we need to talk," Tenley said.

"We can talk and ride," he said.

She nodded, impatient to get to the subject at hand—Alex Stamos. When her grandfather returned, bundled against the cold, Tenley helped him into the sleigh, then handed him the reins.

"Oh, this brings back fine memories," he said, urging the horse into a slow walk. "How long has it been since we've had a ride? Last year, we barely had snow. And the year before that, I spent most of the winter in California with your father. Three years? My, time really does fly."

"Grandpa, I need your help. There's this man—"

"Is someone giving you trouble, Tennie? It's not Randy, is it? Is he making a pest of himself again?"

"No. It's not Randy." Randy Schmitt had been pursuing her since high school and she'd been fending off his affections for just as long.

Tenley fiddled with the fingers of her gloves, searching for a way to enlist her grandfather's help. It wasn't difficult to predict his reaction to her dilemma. But she couldn't think of any way to make Alex's offer sound insignificant.

"I made a little comic book for Josh as a Christmas gift. Just a story with some pictures to go with it. And he loved it so much, he sent it to a publisher in Chicago. Now that publisher has come here, hoping to put the work under contract."

"Tennie, that's fabulous! I didn't realize you were working on your art."

She groaned. "I don't have any art. This was just…doodling. Crude illustrations. The problem is, Josh told the publisher the book was done by T. J. Marshall. And the publisher, his name is Alex Stamos, thinks that's you. So tomorrow, he's going to come by the gallery and try to convince you to sell him the rights to the book. And you're going to tell him you're not interested."

Her grandfather scowled, his eyes still fixed on the road ahead. "Why would you want me to do that? This is your chance to do something on your own. Tennie, you have to grab an opportunity like this. Not many artists can make a living off their talents."

Tenley shook her head. "But I don't have any talent. And I'm just too busy with my work at the gallery."

"You can do both."

"I've never really thought about a career as an artist," she said.

"You've never really thought about a career, period," he said, drawing the horse to a stop at the corner. "Everything went to hell before you had a chance to decide what you wanted to do with your life. You've been afraid to be passionate about anything, Tennie. Afraid if you showed any interest, it would be taken away. But your talent can't be taken away. It's in your genes."

She really had no excuse. Her grandfather was right. But she'd never wanted a career as an artist. She wasn't prepared. "I love my life exactly the way it is."

He shook his head. "No, you don't. Every day, I look at you trying to avoid living, trying to keep things on an even keel. You hide out in that old cabin. You hide behind that makeup and that silly hairdo. You dress yourself in black, as if you're still in mourning. Everything you do is meant to push people away. It's time to take a chance."

He was talking about her art, but what her grandfather said applied to Alex as well—or to men, in general. Reward didn't come without risk. She slipped her arm through his and rested her head on his shoulder. "I don't mean to be such a mess," she said.

Her grandfather laughed. "You've always been a bother. But that's why I love you, Tennie. We're not so different, you and I. I was lucky to find your grandmother. She was a sensible woman and she put me in my place. And I loved her for it. I'd like to think there's someone out there who can do the same for you. Someone who can bring you balance."

Tenley sighed, her breath clouding in front of her face. "Do you ever wonder what he would have been like? He would have changed as he got older. I always try to imagine what kind of man he would have become."

"I know one thing. He would have been mad as hell to see you wasting away in that cabin. He would have told you to get off your butt and make something out of your life."

"He would have," Tenley said with a weak laugh. She gave his arm a squeeze. "Would it be all right if we cut our ride short? I have some things I need to do."

"Sure, sweetheart." He handed her the reins. "I'm going to walk from here. I need some exercise. And I want you to think about what I've said. Carpe diem. Seize the day, Tenley Marshall."

He jumped down to the ground, then knocked on the side of the sleigh. Tenley clucked her tongue and sent Minnie into motion. Though she could have taken a quick way out of town, she decided to ride past the inn.

She slowed the sleigh as she stared up at the window of Alex's room. What was he doing now? Was he lying on the bed, thinking about the time they'd spent together? Was he reliving all of the most passionate moments between them?

She fought the urge to park her sleigh and climb the trellis to the second-story porch that fronted his room. But someone would see the sleigh and question what she was doing at the inn. There'd be all sorts of speculation. Though small-town life could be nice, there was a lot of bad with the good.

"Get up, Minnie," she called. "Let's go home."

Tomorrow would be soon enough to tend to her future. For now, she wanted a quiet place to think about the past twenty-four hours.

THE WHITE CLAPBOARD inn was as quaint on the inside as it was on the exterior. Two huge parlors flanked the entry hall and a wide, open staircase led to the second floor and Alex's room.

Tenley had been right about the choice. The room, furnished with a mix of real and reproduction antiques, was spacious, but cozy. It overlooked a wide upper porch with two sets of French doors that could be thrown open in the warm weather.

After checking in, he'd walked down to a small coffee shop and had dinner, then spent a half-hour looking for a place to buy a new pair of shoes for his meeting with T. J. Marshall. The only men's shop in town was closed and wouldn't open until ten the next morning, so Alex decided to return to his room.

An attempt to kick back and relax only made him more restless. He felt imprisoned amongst the chintz curtains and the overstuffed furniture, used to the soothing mix of rustic charm and natural comfort in Tenley's cabin.

Alex opened the French doors and let the cold wind blow through his room, breathing deeply as he tried to clear his head. Maybe Tenley had it right all along. Maybe people weren't supposed to live with all those silly conveniences like televisions and clocks and microwave ovens.

Though he'd only spent a day with her, Alex sensed something inside him had changed. He looked at his surroundings with a greater awareness of what was necessary for happiness and what could be discarded. And in his mind, Tenley was standing with the necessities.

He looked over at the bed, to the pages of the novel that he'd spread over the surface, the papers fluttering. Tenley. Something had been nagging at him since he'd left her place, something he couldn't quite put his finger on. He locked the doors against the wind and then crossed the room.

His thoughts focused on the drawings he'd found inside her grandfather's books, the little sketches that seemed familiar in a way. Gathering up the pages, Alex stretched out on the bed and began to read the novel again, carefully studying each illustration before moving on.

The haze of desire that had clouded his thoughts slowly cleared and Alex realized instantly what had been bothering him. The heroine in the story was Tenley. A girl who'd lost her family in a tragic accident and who had discovered a way to bring them back to life. Cyd was Tenley. But it was more than that.

The story was so personal, so rooted in the heroine's viewpoint that it could never have been written by a man. Nor had it been illustrated by Tenley's grandfather. She'd done the drawings. And she'd written the story.

He rifled through the pages until he found a close-up of Cyd's hand. The rings that Tenley wore were exactly the same as Cyd's. The shape of the hands, the long, tapered fingers and the black nail polish. Hands just like those that had touched his body and made him ache with need.

"Oh, hell," he muttered, flopping back against the

pillows. This was all his fault. He'd made some rather big assumptions about T. J. Marshall—pretty sexist assumptions—that had been completely wrong. He was looking for an artist by that name from Sawyer Bay and he'd found one. But he'd never considered that the *T* in T.J. might stand for Tenley.

Alex tried to rationalize his mistake. He'd been blinded by desire, anxious to believe everything she said and even things she didn't say. "The surprises never end," he said.

Tenley had never claimed to be a conventional girl, but what artist wouldn't want to make a living from their work? There were thousands upon thousands who struggled to make ends meet every day. And he was offering her a chance to do what she loved and get paid to do it.

Alex carefully straightened the pages, then put them back in his briefcase. As he closed it, he noticed the phone and considered calling her and demanding the truth. But if she'd gone to so much trouble to hide herself from him, then he'd have to proceed cautiously. She'd be the one to sign the contract, so his approach would have to change.

Her number was in the phone book under Tenley J. Thomas J. followed immediately after, and below that, the Marshall Gallery. Had he bothered to look in the phone book, he might have figured this out sooner. And maybe he wouldn't have made the mistake of sleeping with her.

Or maybe not, Alex mused. She would have been

awfully difficult to resist, all soft and naked, her hands skimming over his body. He punched in the digits of her number, casting aside the images that raced through his head, then waited as her phone rang. He wasn't sure what he intended to say or how he intended to say it. But that became a moot point when she didn't answer. "She's probably outside, chopping wood or rebuilding the engine on her Jeep," he muttered.

Irritated, Alex stripped off his shirt and tossed it onto a nearby chair, then discarded his khakis and his socks. The simplest way to occupy his mind was to lose himself in his work, but he preferred to think about Tenley instead. Perhaps a hot shower would clear his head.

He strode to the bathroom and turned on the water, waiting for it to heat up. Then he skimmed his boxers off and stepped inside the tiled stall. Bracing his hands on the wall, he let the water sluice over his neck and back, his eyes closed, his mind drifting.

Tantalizing images teased at his brain and he thought about the sauna, about the two of them naked and sweating, of Tenley's mouth on his shaft and the orgasm that followed. Alex groaned. Just the mere thought brought an unwelcome reaction.

If he got hard every time he thought of her, then he needed to find something else to occupy his mind. He reached for the faucet and turned off the hot water, forcing himself to bear the sting of the cold. It wouldn't take much to ease his predicament and Alex considered taking matters into his own hands. But surrendering wasn't an option. He was the one in control of his desires, not her.

He tipped his face up into the spray, waiting for the water to have an effect on his body. But his mind once again drifted to thoughts of Tenley. What would they be doing at this very moment if he'd spent the night in her cabin? Would they be curled up in front of the fire, drinking hot cocoa? Maybe they'd already be sound asleep, naked in each other's arms, after a long afternoon of mind-blowing sex.

Alex slowly began to count backward from one hundred, challenging his body to bear the cold shower. He needed to stop thinking about sex. Even if he wanted to return to her bed, he didn't have a car. There was no way to get back to her cabin. Hell, he didn't even know where her cabin was.

Finally, after his erection had completely subsided, Alex shut off the water and grabbed a towel from the rack above the toilet. His skin was prickled with goose bumps and he shivered uncontrollably. But his erection was gone.

Alex shook his head, then stepped out of the shower and wrapped the towel around his waist. As he walked back into the room, his ran his hands over his wet chest. But when he glanced up, he jerked in surprise. "Geez, you scared me."

Tenley sat on the edge of the bed, dressed in her parka and fur hat, her big boots dripping water on the hardwood floor.

"How the hell did you get in here?"

She pointed to the French doors. "I climbed up the trellis and came across the porch."

"Those doors are locked."

She shrugged. "They are. But you can jimmy the lock with a library card." Tenley reached in her pocket and pulled out her card. "It's good for more than just books."

Alex stared at her from across the room, afraid to approach for fear that he wouldn't be able to keep his hands off her. Why was she here? Had she missed him as much as he'd missed her?

"I didn't want to sleep alone tonight," she said. "I thought maybe I could sleep here."

"Just sleep?"

Tenley nodded. "I like sleeping with you. When I sleep with you, I don't dream."

Alex knew once they crawled into bed, there'd be a lot more than sleeping on the menu. "Tenley, I think you and I both know that we can't be in the same bed together and just sleep."

"We could try," she said.

Every instinct in Alex's mind and body told him to show her the door. He had an obligation to treat her as a business prospect and the last time he checked, that didn't include losing himself in the warmth of her body. "I'm not even remotely interested in doing that," he said.

Her eyes went wide and he saw the hurt there. "You aren't?"

Alex knew he was risking everything, but suddenly business didn't matter. He could live without her novel, but he couldn't go another minute without her body. "If you spend the night here, I won't hold back." He paused, then decided he might as well be completely honest. Then the ball would be in her court. "I'm going to see your grandfather tomorrow. If he isn't the one who made that story, I'm not going to give up. I'm going to find that person, whoever he—or *she*—is."

She stood, her expression unflinching, and shrugged out of her jacket, letting it drop to the floor at her feet. Then she kicked off her boots and dropped them in front of the door. She still wore the goofy hat with the earflaps. Alex reached out and took it off her head, then set it on the desk.

He hadn't seen her in a few hours, but the effect that her beauty had on his brain was immediate and intense. His gaze drifted from her eyes to her lips. Alex fought the temptation to grab her and pull her down onto the bed, to kiss her until her body went soft beneath his.

Slowly, she removed each piece of clothing, her gaze fixed on his, never faltering. When she was left in just her T-shirt and panties, Alex realized that he hadn't drawn a decent breath since she'd begun. A wave of dizziness caused him to reach out and grab the bedpost.

His fingers twitched with the memory of touching her body as he took in the outline of her breasts beneath the thin cotton shirt. He looked down to see his reaction, becoming more evident through the damp towel. Tenley noticed as well, her gaze lingering on his crotch.

Who were they trying to fool? There was no way they'd crawl into bed together and not enjoy the pleasures of the flesh. Alex untwisted the towel from his waist and it dropped to the floor. Then he pulled her into his arms, tumbling them both back onto the bed.

This was dangerous, he thought to himself as he drew her leg up along his hip. To need a woman so much that it defied all common sense was something he'd never experienced in the past. It wasn't a bad feeling, just a very scary situation. How much was he willing to give up to possess her? And when would it be enough?

TENLEY STARED at the landscape of the harbor at Gill's Rock. "It's lovely," she said, nodding. "The colors are softer than those you used on the painting of Detroit harbor. Are you going to have prints made?"

"Definitely. The prints of Fish Creek harbor sold well. I'm thinking we ought to do some smaller ones and sell the whole series as a package."

"Are there any harbors left to do?"

"After Jackson, I think I'm done with them," her grandfather said. "I'm going to move on to barns. Or log buildings."

"You could start with the cabin."

"I was thinking of doing that. But there's a nice barn on Clark's Lake Road that I've always wanted to paint." He stepped back, studying his painting intently. "Lighthouses, harbors, barns. The tourists love them and I do give them what they love."

Tenley knew the compromises that her grandfather had to make over the course of his life. Though he might have wanted to become a serious painter and have his work hang in museums, he'd come to accept his talent for what it was—good enough to provide for his wife and a family and more than enough to tempt the tourists into buying.

"By the way," her grandfather said, "I like the new look. All that stuff on your eyes…I never understood that. You're a pretty girl, Tennie." He paused. "No, you're a beautiful woman."

Tenley threw her arms around his neck and gave him a fierce hug. "I have to run over to the post office. I think your paints are here. And I'm going to mail these bills, too. Do you have anything you want to put in?"

Her grandfather scowled. "Is there a reason you're so anxious to leave?"

"No. I just have work to do."

"I thought you said that guy from the publishing house was going to stop by."

Tenley wasn't sure what Alex had planned for the day. She'd slipped out of his room at dawn, leaving him sound asleep, his naked body tangled in the sheets, his dark hair mussed. To her relief, she'd managed to crawl back down the trellis and get back her Jeep without anyone seeing her, minimizing the chances for gossip.

"He might. He didn't make an appointment, so I don't know what time he plans to show up. If he comes, tell him I'll be back soon."

"Tenley, I am not going to make excuses for you. The man has come all the way from Chicago. The least you could do is talk to him."

Oh, she'd done a whole lot more than talk to him already, Tenley mused. If her grandfather only knew the naughty things he'd done to her, he'd probably lock the front door of the gallery and call Harvey Willis to escort Alex out of town. "I'll only be a few minutes, so—"

The bell above the gallery door jingled and she heard someone step inside. Tenley forced a smile. "There he is," she said. Clutching the envelopes in front of her, she wandered out of the workroom and into the showroom. Alex stood at the door, dressed in a sport jacket, a crisp blue shirt and dark wool trousers. His hair was combed and he'd shaved and he looked nothing like the man she'd left that morning.

"Hello," she said, unable to hide a smile. There were times when she forgot just how handsome he was. Boys like Alex had always been way out of her league. They dated the popular girls, the girls who worried about clothes and hair and...boobs. They always had boobs. Tenley glanced down at her chest, then crossed her arms over her rather unremarkable breasts.

"Hi. I'm here to see T. J. Marshall."

Tenley swallowed hard. It was now or never. Her grandfather wouldn't take part in the subterfuge, so Tenley was faced with only one choice. She cleared her throat and straightened to her full height. "I'm T. J. Marshall. At least, I'm the one you're looking for."

He didn't seem surprised. "Yeah, I kind of figured that out on my own." He crossed the room and held out his hand. "Alex Stamos. Stamos Publishing."

Hesitantly, she placed her fingers in his palm. The instant they touched, she felt a tremor race through her. He slowly brought her hand to his lips and pressed a kiss to her fingertips. "I missed you this morning," he whispered. "I woke up and you weren't there."

"See, that wasn't so difficult."

Tenley jumped at the sound of her grandfather's voice. She tugged her hand from Alex's and fixed a smile on her face. "Alex Stamos, this is my grandfather, Thomas Marshall. Also known as T.J. Or Tom."

Alex held his hand out. "It's a pleasure to meet you, sir. You have a very talented granddaughter. Did she tell you we're interested in publishing her graphic novel?"

"I've always thought she had talent. She used to draw little sketches in all my books. Drove me crazy. I thought she might be an illustrator someday. She never did like books without pictures." He chuckled softly. "Well, it's a pleasure, Alex. I'll leave you two to your business."

When they were alone, Alex reached out for her hand again, placing it on his chest. "Why did you leave?"

"I figured I'd better get out of there or the whole town would be talking."

Alex gave her fingers a squeeze. "So, what do you think they'd say if I took you to breakfast? There's a nice little coffee shop down the street from the inn."

"You didn't stay for the cinnamon rolls?"

He shook his head. "Hmm. Cinnamon rolls. Tenley. Cinnamon rolls. Tenley. The choice wasn't tough."

"All right," she said. "But you're buying."

"I wouldn't have it any other way."

Tenley grabbed her jacket and they stepped out into

the chilly morning. "How did you figure it out?" she asked as they headed away from the harbor.

"I was flipping through some of those books your grandfather mentioned. There were drawings in the margins. At first I thought they were just crude scribblings, but then I came across one that looked very familiar."

Tenley knew she ought to apologize. But that might prompt a discussion of her motives and even she wasn't sure why she'd kept her real identity a secret from him. "I didn't intend to deceive you. I just didn't want anything to… I wanted to be able to… I wasn't ready…" She shook her head, feeling her cheeks warm with embarrassment. "It's sometimes easier not to get too personal. At least, that's always worked for me in the past."

"So, I'm just one in a long line of uninformed men?" he asked.

Her breath caught in her throat. "No! You're not like anyone I've every known. I thought if you knew, you wouldn't want to sleep with me." She cursed softly. "I wanted you and you wanted me. All that other stuff is just…business."

"I have rules about mixing business with pleasure. Very strict rules."

"You haven't mixed the two. Not yet."

"What are you talking about?"

She straightened. "I haven't agreed to do business with you, Alex, so all we've had is the pleasure part. You haven't broken any rules…yet."

Alex laughed, shaking his head. "Whatever made me think this was going to be easy? God, I thought I'd come up here, do my little presentation, charm you and get you to sign on the dotted line."

"You have charmed me," she said.

"Yeah, I've heard I have a way with women," he muttered. "But do me a favor. Don't say no until I've told you the plan. Consider my offer and if you don't like it, then I'll—I'll make you another offer." He stopped and grabbed her arms, turning her to face him. "But be assured of one thing, Tenley. You are going to sign with me."

"You must have a lot of confidence in that charm of yours," Tenley said.

"It worked on you, didn't it?"

"I think you're forgetting who seduced whom." She started walking again, then turned back to him. "Maybe I should hire an agent. Just to make sure I get the best deal."

"At least an agent would make sure you didn't pass on a great deal. He'd say, don't be stupid. Sign the contract."

In truth, Tenley *was* interested in how much her novel might bring. After talking with her grandfather, she'd begun to see the wisdom in his words. She'd be silly to turn down a chance to make money from her art. But she had no idea what a project like hers was worth. There was the money to discuss—and a few other conditions.

"But an agent will take fifteen percent," he added. "You don't need an agent. I'm going to give you a good offer." He caught up to her as they turned down the main street, toward the inn. "I had a nice time last night. Did you sleep well?"

Tenley nodded. "I did."

"I'm going to stay another night," he said.

"I thought you'd be leaving today."

Alex took her hand and tucked it into the crook of his arm. "Nope. I'm going to stay until I convince you to sign with us. And after that, we're going to go over all the things that need to be done with your story to make it better."

When they reached the coffee shop, Alex opened the door for her and stepped aside for her to enter. The shop was filled with all the usual customers. Morning coffee was a daily ritual for a number of the folks in town, choosing the same seats every day.

Her entrance caused a quite a stir, with everyone turning to watch as the hostess seated them in a booth near the front windows. She handed them menus and asked about coffee. Alex ordered a cup and Tenley asked for orange juice.

"Why is everyone staring?" Alex whispered.

"I don't usually come in here," Tenley said. "It's like Gossip Central. If you want the town to know your business, you just mention it during breakfast at The Coffee Bean. Here, information moves faster than the Internet."

They ordered breakfast, Tenley choosing a huge platter with three eggs, bacon, hash browns, a biscuit and three small pancakes. Alex settled for toast and coffee.

"Not hungry?" she asked.

"I usually have a bigger lunch," he said. "So, I think we need to talk business."

"Let's not," Tenley said, slathering her biscuit with honey. She took a huge bite and grinned at him. "Sex always makes me hungry. I find that my appetite is in direct proportion to the intensity of my orgasms. This morning I am really, really hungry. You should be, too. We did it three times—no wait, four times, last night. That has to be some kind of record."

Alex glanced around. "Do you really think this is an appropriate topic for breakfast conversation?"

Tenley slipped her foot out of her boot and wriggled her toes beneath his pant leg. "You know what I like the best? I like the way you look, right before you come. Your lip twitches and you get this really intense expression on your face. I love that expression."

She loved the way his body tensed and flexed as he moved inside of her, she loved the feel of his skin beneath her fingers and the warmth of his mouth on hers. Tenley loved that she could make him lose touch with reality for a few brief moments. There weren't many things that she did well, but seducing Alex was one task at which she excelled.

Alex cleared his throat. "Stop."

"Why?"

"Because I don't like being teased, especially in public."

She took another bite of her biscuit and then held it out to him. "You should eat more. You're going to need your energy. We should go skiing. Have you ever been cross-country skiing?"

"Never," Alex said.

"Or skating. There's a nice rink in Sister Bay. And you can rent skates. Do you know how to skate?"

"I used to play hockey when I was a kid. But I'm not much for the cold. I prefer warm-weather activities. I like windsurfing. I go hiking. I like to water-ski."

"We have all that here. Just not now."

"Tenley, I want to talk about this contract."

"Always about business," she muttered. "I find business very dull. And if you're trying to charm me, you're not doing a very good job. If I want to go skating, then you should be happy to take me."

"I don't have anything to wear," he said.

"We have stores here. You'll need some long underwear and a decent pair of boots. And some good gloves. Those leather gloves won't last. We'll go shopping after breakfast."

It was nice to have a playmate, both in and out of bed. Alex made a good companion. He was funny and easygoing and he seemed to find her amusing. And he made her shudder with pleasure whenever he touched her. What more could a girl want?

She grabbed a piece of bacon from her plate and slowly munched on it. With Tommy's death, she'd lost her best friend. Since then, she hadn't tried to find a new one. Alex was the first person she really wanted to spend time with.

"All right," he said. "We'll talk business at dinner."

"At my place," she said. "I'll cook."

"You're not going to distract me again," he said. "I want you to promise. And I think it would be better if we went out."

Tenley shrugged. "We'll see."

"If you don't promise, I'm going to kiss you, right here and now." He glanced around. "What would the gossips say about that?"

"Go ahead," Tenley said. "I dare you." In truth, she wanted him to accept the challenge. She wanted to shock everyone watching, to make them wonder just what poor, pitiful Tenley Marshall was doing with this sexy stranger.

When he didn't make a move, she leaned across the table, took his face in her hands and gave Alex a long, lingering kiss. She didn't bother to look at the crowd's reaction. Tenley chose to enjoy the look on Alex's face, instead. "I don't make a dare unless I'm willing to back it up."

He licked his lips, then grinned. "Bacon," he murmured. Reaching out, he snatched a piece from her plate. "Maybe I'm hungrier than I thought."

5

ALEX CURLED INTO Tenley's naked body, pulling her against him and tucking her backside into his lap. He usually didn't spend a lot of time outdoors during the winter. But since he'd come to Door County, he'd realized just how delicious it felt to spend the day outside in the cold and the evening getting warm in bed.

Though this had begun as a business trip, it was slowly transforming into one of the best vacations he'd ever had. Previous vacations had always been solitary escapes, a time to get away from his social life and focus on himself. But his time with Tenley was making him question why he hadn't enjoyed those holidays in the company of a woman.

Perhaps because he didn't really know any women who shared his interests. The girls he dated weren't really interested in hiking the mountains or rafting river rapids. But Tenley had probably experienced more of those things than he had. "Are you awake?" he whispered.

"Umm. Just barely."

"What do you think of rock climbing?"

"Right now?" she asked.

"No, in general."

"It's difficult to do in the winter," she said. "Cold hands, slippery rocks, big boots. But there are some nice spots around here if you come back in the summer. We could go." She rolled over to face him. Her hands smoothed over his chest and she placed a kiss at the base of his neck. "You should try kayaking. And hiking at Rock Island is fun. But that's all summer stuff. We could snowshoe. Have you ever been snowshoeing? I'll take you tomorrow if you'd like."

"Interesting," he said.

"It is." She sighed, then rolled on top of him, stretching her naked body along the length of his. "And then there's sex. Sex is a year-round thing in Door County." Her lips found his and she gave him a sweet kiss.

Was it possible she was the perfect woman? He'd always imagined his ideal mate to be tall and blonde and eager to please. And though Tenley did excel in the bedroom, she did it on her own terms. There was no question about who was in control. Maybe he'd been looking for the wrong perfect woman.

"Is there anything you wouldn't try?" he asked.

"Scuba diving," she said. "Being underwater scares me. It would be like drowning alive."

Well, there it was. She wasn't perfect. Alex loved scuba diving. "Interesting," he said.

"You know what would be *really* interesting? If you'd get up and make dinner for us."

"Don't you think you're taking this slave-boy thing

a bit too far? Just because I want that contract, doesn't mean you can take advantage of me."

She sat up and clapped her hands, her face lighting up with amusement. "Oh, a slave boy. I've always wanted one of those. I think that's a wonderful idea." Tenley crawled over the covers until she was stretched out alongside him, her head at his feet. She wiggled her toes. "Rub my feet, slave boy."

Alex let his gaze drift along her naked body. Would he ever get enough of her? Though he'd only known her for a few days, he'd come to think of her body as his, as if he were the only one smart enough to see what an incredible woman she was.

Grabbing her foot, he rubbed his thumbs against her arch. "How's that?"

"Oh, that feels so nice."

He pressed his lips to a spot beneath her ankle. "How about that?"

"That's nice, too. But don't stop rubbing."

"So, let me tell you about what we can do for your novel."

"Please don't. I just want to relax. Talking about business makes me nervous."

"Do you plan to fight me on this every step of the way? If this is some plan to drive me crazy so I'll leave, it's not going to work."

"Would sex work?" she asked.

"Sex?"

"Yes. If I seduced you right now, would you be satisfied?"

"I'm always satisfied when you seduce me." Alex picked up her other foot. "What are you afraid of, Tenley? Most artists would jump at the chance to sell their work."

"I don't really know what I'm doing," she said. "I didn't go to art school. I haven't studied writing. I have no technique, no style. I'm afraid if I have to produce something, I'll just…freak out."

"You don't seem like the type to freak out. Besides, some of the greatest writers and artists never went to college. So that excuse doesn't fly. What else?"

"That story was personal. What if I only have one story in me? And now that it's out, there's nothing left."

"No problem. We'll cross that bridge when we come to it. For now, we'll focus on the novel you have written. Anything else?"

"Are you going to work on this book with me?"

"Yes. You'll also have an editor to work with once the contract is signed. But if you want me to stay involved, I will. This imprint is my idea, so I am going to have my fingers in it until it gets up and running."

"So, you and I will be…business associates? And we'll pretend that we've never seen each other naked. And that we've never touched each other in intimate ways."

He chuckled. "That's going to be very difficult to forget."

She sat up, crossing her legs in front of her and resting her arms on her knees. "But how will it work, when I see you? Don't you think it will be strange?"

Alex saw the confusion in her eyes. "Because we've been lovers? I don't know. I guess we're just going to have to make it up as we go along."

To be honest with himself, Alex hadn't really thought about the end of their affair. He wasn't sure why it had to end. The passion they'd shared was real and intense, not something that could be tossed aside without a second thought.

Was Tenley worried she was about to become another notch on his bedpost? Like all those other women who'd registered their complaints on that silly Web site? Sure, he didn't have the best reputation, but where was it written that a guy couldn't change?

"Tenley, I want to get to know you better. I don't want to think this will be over when I go back to Chicago."

A tiny smile twitched at her lips. "Me neither."

"Then let's do it. Let's get to know each other. You start. Ask me any question and I'll answer it. Go ahead."

She regarded him shrewdly. "All right. Do you want to have sex with me all the time, or are there times when you're thinking about something else?"

Alex laughed. This was one instance when he wasn't afraid to be honest. "When you're in the room, I'm pretty much thinking about the next time I'll see you naked. And when you're not close by, I'm thinking about the next time I'll be with you—so I can take off your clothes and see you naked."

"Men think about sex a lot, don't they? Women aren't supposed to think about it."

"Do you?"

"Yes," she said, her voice filled with astonishment. "All the time. When I see you dressed, the first thing I want to do is take your clothes off. I like the way you look. I like your skin and your muscles and your eyes and your hair."

"My turn. Tell me about your favorite fantasy."

Her face softened and her expression grew wistful. "That one is easy. I'm at work and I'm sitting at my desk and the bell above the door rings and there he is. All grown up. He still looks the same, but he's bigger. And it's like it never happened, like he was just gone for a few hours, running errands or having lunch."

He'd expected a sexual fantasy, at least that was what he thought they were talking about. But from the look on her face, he could see the emotional toll the confession was taking. He wanted to stop her, to tell her she misunderstood, yet he was curious to know the truth.

"Your brother?"

She nodded. "I used to have that dream all the time. It would be the only thing that kept the nightmares from becoming unbearable. I'd wake up and I'd be so happy. Sometimes, it was different. I'd be somewhere and I'd see him on the street and I'd run after him. Or I'd be hiking and find him sitting in the woods, all alone."

"What happened, Tenley? How did he die?"

She bit her bottom lip. Her voice wavered when she spoke. "Tommy drowned. In a boating accident," she said. "I'm getting hungry. I think you should fetch us some dinner."

He kissed her gently, satisfied that she'd told him enough for now. "I'm not much of a cook."

"There's a bar in town that makes the best pizza. We can order one and you can go pick it up. And while you're gone, I'll feed the horses and make a fire. Then after supper, we'll take a walk down to the bay."

"That sounds good to me," he said, dropping a kiss on her lips. "And then we'll talk about your book."

"What if I just say 'yes' right now? Then do we have to talk about it tonight?"

"Are you saying yes?" Alex asked.

Tenley nodded. "Yes. Yes, you may publish my silly book, Alex. Yes, I'll sign your contract. As long as we don't have to talk about it for the rest of the night."

Alex held out his hand. "Deal." He paused. "Don't shake unless you mean it. A verbal agreement is legal and binding."

She shook his hand. "Deal. Green olives, green peppers, sausage and mushrooms. And get the eighteen-inch. With extra cheese. And hot peppers on the side."

"Can I get dressed first?" he asked.

Tenley rolled over onto her stomach, her legs crossed at the ankles. "As long as I can watch. But do it really slowly."

He got up and began to retrieve his clothes from where they were scattered on the floor. Tenley followed his movements, a brazen grin on her face. "Stop staring at me," he teased, repeating the words she'd said to him their first night together.

"In the summer, I live without clothes."

"Really?"

"I walk down to the bay and climb down the cliffs and take off all my clothes and lie on the rocks in the sun. Sometimes sailboats go by and see me, but I don't care."

Alex could picture her, walking through the forest like a wood nymph, her long, pale limbs moving gracefully through the lush undergrowth. He'd be back in the summer to see that, making a silent promise to himself.

"Why don't you come with me to this bar? We'll eat there. Maybe have a few drinks. Then we'll come back and I'll help you feed the horses."

"Would this be a date?" Tenley asked.

"Yes," Alex said. "This would be a date."

"Then I accept," she said. She jumped up and ran from the bedroom to the bathroom. "I'll have to make myself pretty."

"No," he said. "I like you just the way you are." There was nothing at all he'd want to change about Tenley. And Alex found that fact quite amazing.

TENLEY GRABBED the pitcher of beer from the bar and walked over to the table she and Alex had chosen. He followed behind her with two empty glasses and a basket of popcorn. Before she sat down, he pulled her chair out for her and Tenley sent him a playful smile.

"Your mother taught you well," she said.

"My great-grandmother," he corrected. "She was from the old country. She learned English by reading Emily Post and she somehow got the idea that all

Americans had to act that way. Usually Greek families are loud and boisterous. We're loud, but unfailingly polite. You should hear our conversation around the table at Easter."

"My parents didn't believe in social conventions. They let us run wild. We were allowed to say and do anything we wanted. As I look back on it, I'm not sure that was good. It's cute in children, but people think it's weird in adults."

"I think you turned out just fine," Alex said.

Tenley loved the little compliments he paid her. She'd often thought a good boyfriend would work hard to make her happy. And Alex seemed to do that naturally, as if his only thought was to please her. "Do you have a girlfriend?" she asked.

The words just popped out of her mouth and an instant later, she wanted to take the question back. Yet her curiosity overwhelmed her. How could a guy like Alex be single? He was smart and funny and gorgeous. And there were a lot of women in Chicago who would consider him a great catch.

"No," he replied. "I don't really get into long-term relationships. I date a lot of different women, but no one seriously."

"I see," Tenley said. Though it was exactly what she wanted to hear—he was unattached—she wasn't sure she liked the fact that he dated "a lot" of women. Was she just the latest of many? "But do you sleep with them?"

"On occasion," he said in a measured tone. "What about you?"

"I don't sleep with women, especially women who've dated you. Although there was a rumor going around town that I preferred girls."

"Do you?" Alex asked.

"I started the rumor. I got tired of every single man in town asking me out. I don't think there's anything wrong with liking girls. You love who you love. I guess if you're lucky enough to find that, it shouldn't make a difference."

"I guess not," Alex said. "I've been thinking that I might be missing out. Maybe I should try the whole relationship thing. See how it goes."

"I wouldn't be any good at that," Tenley said. "I have too much baggage. Everyone says so. They say my last name should be Samsonite."

Alex laughed, but Tenley had never found the comment particularly funny. She couldn't help how she felt. Putting on a sunny face and pretending she was happy seemed like a waste of energy.

But this was the first time she'd been out in ages, and she was with a man she found endlessly intriguing. And tonight, they'd go home and crawl into her bed and make love. Tenley had to admit, for the first time in a long time, she was genuinely happy.

"Who is that guy over there?" Alex asked, pointing toward the bar. "He's giving me the evil eye."

Tenley glanced over her shoulder, then moaned. "Oh, that's Randy. He's in love with me."

"Really?" Alex's eyebrow shot up. "He doesn't seem like your type."

"He thinks he's in love with me," Tenley corrected. "He's had a crush on me since high school and every year about this time, he asks me out to the Valentine's Day dance at the firehouse. And every year, I say no."

"You'd think he'd get the message," Alex said.

"He's kind of thick-headed," Tenley explained. She looked at Randy again, then quickly turned around. "He's coming over here. Maybe we should leave."

"No!" Alex said. "We have just as much right to be here as he does. Besides, I'm hungry and they haven't brought our pizza yet."

"Hello, Tenley."

She forced a smile as she looked up. He really wasn't such a bad guy. Except for the fact that he was in love with her. "Hello, Randy."

He shifted nervously, back and forth on his feet. "How have you been doing? I haven't seen you in a while. I heard you had breakfast at the Bean this morning. I thought you didn't like that place."

"News travels fast." Randy had probably heard about the kiss as well, but Tenley wasn't going to get into that. "Randy, this is Alex Stamos. Alex, Randy Schmitt."

Alex got to his feet and held out his hand, but Randy refused to take it, turning his attention back to Tenley. "Can I talk to you for a second?"

"Randy, I'm not sure that—"

"Just for a second. Over there." He pointed to the far end of the bar.

Tenley looked at Alex and he shrugged. "All right." She pushed back in her chair and stood. "Just for a second."

Randy held on to her elbow as they wove through the patrons at the restaurant. Tenley was aware of the gazes that followed them and she knew what they were thinking. It was the opinion of most of the folks in town that Randy was just about the only man who'd be interested in marrying Tenley Marshall. Though Tenley had never given him any encouragement, he persisted with his belief that they were destined to be together.

In truth, Tenley felt a bit sorry for Randy. It must be horrible to love someone who couldn't love you back. She'd made sure to harden her heart against love, but Randy wore his on his sleeve.

"What are you doing with that guy?"

"It's not what you think," she said. "He's just a friend."

"A friend you kiss at the breakfast table. And rumor has it that he spent the night out at your place. Jesse said he pulled the guy's car out of the ditch after you took him home. Now, I can understand that a girl like you might be attracted to a big-city guy like him, but he's all wrong for you, Tenley. He won't make you happy the way I will."

"Randy, you have to give this up. I don't love you. I'm not going to suddenly change my mind one day and marry you. You need to find someone else."

"I know those flatlanders," he said. "They flash around their money and think they can take whatever they want."

His attitude wasn't uncommon. Though the locals appreciated the money that tourists brought in, they didn't like them encroaching on their territory—especially their women.

"Randy, I'm going to go back and sit down. I suggest you finish your beer and go home."

"Hell, no! I've been waiting around for you all these years, thinking that sooner or later, you'd get your act together and see what's standing right in front of you. I'm the one who loves you, not him. He'll go back to Chicago and I'll be here. You'll see."

"But I don't love you," Tenley insisted. "I'm sorry." Frustrated, she turned to walk away. But Randy grabbed her arm and wouldn't let go.

"If you'd just give us a chance, I know I could—"

"Hey, buddy, let her go."

Tenley closed her eyes at the sound of Alex's voice. One moment, he'd been watching them from the table and the next, he was behind her. "I knew we should have had pizza at home," she muttered.

Alex grabbed Randy's wrist. "I mean it. Let her go."

"Get the hell out of here," Randy snarled. "You can't tell me what to do. I'm not your goddamned buddy, buddy."

"I will tell you what to do when you're making an ass out of yourself. She's not interested. Didn't you hear her?"

The next few seconds passed in a blur. Randy slapped at Alex's hand and accidentally hit Tenley in the head. Alex shoved Randy, Randy took a swing at Alex, and Tenley reacted. Without thinking, she drew back her fist and hit Randy squarely in the nose.

Blood erupted from his left nostril as he stumbled

back and knocked down a waitress with a tray full of drinks. "I'm sorry, I'm sorry," Tenley cried. "I didn't mean to do that." She held on to Alex to keep him from jumping on top of Randy, yet at the same time tried to help Randy to his feet.

"Tenley Marshall, I'm going to have to take you in." Harvey Willis stepped into the middle of the fight, his considerable girth creating a wall between Alex and Randy. The police chief's napkin was still stuffed in his collar and he was holding his fork in his right hand.

"This was not her fault," Alex protested. "She was just defending herself."

"You pipe down or I'll take you in, too. She wasn't defending herself, she was defending you. Now, I can understand how that might piss Randy off, seeing as how you're not from around here. But punching a guy in the face is assault. And doing it in a restaurant full of people is just bad manners."

"I don't want to press charges," Randy said, holding his flannel shirt up to his nose.

"Well, we'll sort that out down at the station. Tenley, you'll come with me. Your flatlander friend can follow us. Randy, you can walk off the pitcher of beer you drank. The exercise will do you good. Let's go." He nodded to the bartender. "They'll be back later to settle up, Bert. And pack up my pizza for me. I'll send Leroy back to get it."

Tenley struggled into her jacket as she walked out the front door. Harvey's cruiser was parked out front in a No Parking zone. "You can get in front," he said. "I don't think you're going to try any funny business, are you?"

"No," Tenley said. "I don't know why you're blaming me for this. You saw Randy start it. He just won't give up."

When they were both in the car, Harvey turned to her and shook his finger. "Tenley Marshall, you know how that man feels about you. Still, you decide to parade your out-of-state boyfriend in front of him and the whole town. How do you think he's supposed to react?"

"Alex Stamos is not my boyfriend. And I've made it perfectly clear to Randy that I don't have feelings for him. *And,* this is the big one, I didn't realize Randy was there. Had I known, we would have gone somewhere else."

"Well, since this Alex fella has come to town, people have been worried for you. You're not acting the way you usually do."

Tenley's temper flared. "Maybe if everyone would just mind their own business, I could get on with my life."

"Is that what you've been doing? I just think it's a little funny you've been hiding away like a hermit for years and then he rolls into town and you're suddenly a social butterfly. He seems to be the slick sort and you're falling for his tricks."

"Let's go," she muttered. "I'd really like to take care of this before it causes any more gossip."

"Oh, well, I think that horse is out of the barn already," Harvey replied.

They drove the three short blocks to the police station and by the time Tenley got out of the car, Alex was standing at the door, waiting for her, pacing back and forth. "Is she going to need a lawyer?" he asked. "Because if you're going to charge her with anything, then I want to get her a lawyer."

"Oh, just pipe down," Harvey said. "We're going to fill out a report, she's going to pay a fine and then you'll be on your way. We don't tolerate physical violence here, unlike what goes on in the big cities."

"He's the one who grabbed her first. She was trying to get away when I stepped in. And then he took a swing at me."

"I know. I saw the whole thing. So did half the town. But Tenley drew blood, so she's going to have to pay the fine."

As they walked into the lobby, Tenley turned to Alex. "Wait here. I'll be out in a few minutes. And don't start things up again with Randy. He's drunk and he has at least fifty pounds on you. Besides, Harvey treats outsiders a lot more harshly than townies."

True to Harvey's word, the matter was dispatched by filling out a short report and paying a small fine. Since Tenley didn't have fifty dollars in her wallet, Harvey agreed to let her come in the following morning with the money.

By the time they finished, Randy had arrived and was sitting glumly in the reception area across from Alex, staring at him with a sulky expression. Harvey motioned to him and he approached Tenley with a contrite smile. "I don't want to press charges," he insisted.

"Randy, my boy, you need to move on with your life," Harvey said. "Tenley's not interested. There's nothing more pathetic than a guy who won't take no for an answer. You bother her again and I'll toss your ass in jail. By the way, Linda Purnell has been in love with you for going on three years. If I were you, I'd give her a second look." He paused, then directed his gaze at Alex. "As for you, I'm going to be watching you. You keep your nose clean and you and me won't have any problems."

Alex stood and held out his hand to Tenley. "Thank you. We'll just be going now."

When they got outside, Alex dragged her toward his rented SUV. "What the hell was that?"

Tenley laughed. "Next time, when I suggest pizza at home, maybe we should just stay home and forget all this dating stuff."

"No," Alex said stubbornly. "Tomorrow night, we're going on a damn date. And you're going to wear a pretty dress and I'm going to take you to a nice restaurant, and we're going to have a pleasant evening that doesn't involve jealous ex-boyfriends and bloody noses."

"He was not my boyfriend," Tenley insisted.

Alex yanked open the passenger-side door. "Well, I *am* your boyfriend, and if we have to drive to Green Bay to get some privacy, we will."

ALEX STARED OUT the window of the tower studio, taking in the view of the bay beyond the trees. Tenley was seated at the drawing table, a pad of paper in front of her. "All right," she said. "I'm ready. Fire away."

"This isn't supposed to be painful," Alex said. "We're working together on this. To make your novel better."

"Why don't you just give me the list and I'll look it over and we can discuss it later."

"Because I want you to understand what we need before you sign the contract. So there are no misunderstandings."

"Take off your shirt," she said.

Alex cursed beneath his breath. "I'm not going to let you change the subject again, Tenley. Whenever you don't want to do something, you try to seduce me."

"I'm not going to seduce you, I want to try drawing you. So take off your shirt. And the rest of your clothes while you're at it."

"Tenley, this isn't going to get you—"

"Slave boy, you're not listening. I feel the need to draw you and you're supposed to do everything in your power to please me."

This was getting to be a pattern with the two of them, although Alex really couldn't be too upset. What man would grow impatient with a woman who wanted sex as much as he did? They did have the entire day to work on her novel. He could give her an hour or two of forced nudity as long as it was followed by more pleasurable activities.

"First of all, we need to have an understanding," he said. "This can't end up like one of those sex videos that everyone gets to see. This is for your own private viewing pleasure. Agreed? This will not end up on the Internet."

Hell, he'd had enough trouble from scorned girl-friends. Adding naked drawings to the mix would probably send his mother right over the edge.

"I won't even give you a face. Unless people recognize other parts of you, you'll be completely anonymous."

Reluctantly, Alex stripped out of his clothes, then stood and waited while Tenley gathered the things she needed. When she was ready, she took a deep breath. "All right. Turn around and brace your hands against that post. And lean into it."

He did as she ordered. With his back to her, all he could hear was the occasional rustle of paper and a few soft curses from Tenley. His arms were beginning to grow stiff and his shoulders tight when she finally spoke again.

"There. I think I'm done."

He turned around and she held up the sketchpad. Though Alex didn't know a lot about art, he knew the drawing was beautifully rendered, every muscle perfectly shaded. "Wow."

"You're hot," she said. "I'm not sure I got your butt right. But it's a decent first attempt."

"Tenley, it's better than decent. It's very good."

"You really think so?" She stared at the sketch. "You know, I've been thinking maybe I should take some classes. The university in Green Bay has an art program."

With any other woman, he might have turned on the charm and lavished compliments to soothe her insecurities. But as he grew to care about Tenley, Alex realized that they needed to have honesty between them.

"There are great art schools in Chicago, too," he said. "And you're good enough to get into a top-notch program, Tenley. Sure, you haven't had a lot of experience, but you do have talent."

"I couldn't move," she said distractedly, her attention still focused on her sketch. "My grandfather is here. He needs my help. Besides, I have my cabin and my animals. I couldn't bring them to Chicago."

Though Alex had considered what the future might hold for them, he'd never really appreciated her ties to this place. She was living in a paradise and he couldn't blame her for not wanting to leave. He'd only spent a few days here and he didn't want to leave either. What was Chicago compared to the beauty of this place?

"They have seminars at the Art Institute. You could come for a few days. Meet everyone at the office. Maybe do some publicity shots. You could stay with me."

"I want to try another pose," she said, changing the subject. "Turn to the side and lean back against the post." She stared at him for a long moment. "Put your right leg forward a bit and then hold on to the post with your left hand."

For the next hour, she sketched, posing him in different positions and then quickly completing the drawing. She tossed aside the pencil for charcoal and then switched to pastels.

"All right," she finally said. "You can get dressed."

"You're finished?"

Tenley stared at the drawings scattered across her table. "I think I can do this," she said breathlessly. "I'm not as bad as I thought I was."

"You're sure you want me to get dressed?"

Tenley grinned. "Yes. Well, only if you want to. If you prefer to work like that, then you can stay naked."

"We're going to work now?"

"Yes," she said in a gloomy voice. "You're going to tell me what's wrong with my novel and I'm going to try to fix it." She jumped up. "You do need to get dressed. It's too distracting having you sitting around here naked." She walked over to him and smoothed her hand from his belly to his cock.

Alex groaned as he closed his eyes, waiting for the involuntary reaction that came from her touch. Though he wanted nothing more than to make love to her, he had a choice to make. She was willing to talk business now. So sex would have to wait until later.

Turning away from her touch, Alex pulled on his boxers and jeans and then slipped into his shirt, not bothering to button it. "All right. The first thing, and this is going to be big—we're going to have to redraw everything. Your friend has the original, but even that is a little too rough. We're going to print at a high resolution, so everything has to be very clean."

"That's going to take a long time. I'd have to draw it oversized in order to get it just perfect."

"No, we'll scan it into a computer and have our graphic artist clean it up. But there are some parts that will need additional drawings and changes to the story."

Tenley took a deep breath. "Why don't we start with those changes first?"

Alex pulled up a stool and sat down next to her. He grabbed her hand. He pressed a kiss to the back of her wrist. This was actually going to happen. Tenley was going to sell her book to him and he was going to make her famous. He was also going to make her a lot of money. But it wasn't that thought that thrilled him. It was the fact that he and Tenley would always have a connection.

Over the next two hours, they worked together, going over the editor's notes, discussing the production process, arguing about the plot and drawings needed to flesh out the story.

For the first time since Alex arrived, he saw Tenley excited about the possibility of her novel being published. And he was grateful he was the one to make it happen. It was so easy to make her happy. It didn't require a huge bank account or a fancy apartment or the promise of a comfortable life or social status, things the other women he knew were always searching for.

Tenley responded to kindness and encouragement. Something terrible must have happened to make her so unsure of herself, Alex mused. Though he only knew the barest details of her brother's death, he was determined to learn more.

He wanted to know every tiny detail of her life, everything that made her the woman she was. He wanted to be the man who understood her the best. He wanted to be the man she turned to when she felt frightened or overwhelmed or lonely.

Making himself indispensable to Tenley Marshall was a huge task. But Alex was afraid of the consequences if he didn't. For it was becoming more and more evident that Tenley needed to be a permanent part of his life.

6

TENLEY RUBBED her eyes, then pinched them shut. She knew she ought to just set the work aside and get some sleep, but every time she closed her eyes, doubts began to plague her.

It was simple to feel good about herself when Alex was standing behind her, cheering her on. But without him, all her insecurities rushed back. How would she ever do this on her own? Nothing she drew would ever be good enough. She'd always find fault.

Tossing the drawing pad on the floor, she flopped back into the leather sofa. This was entirely his fault. Until she'd taken him home during the storm, she'd been perfectly happy with her life. She found her work at her grandfather's gallery satisfying and her free time was spent in relaxing pursuits, not frantically trying to make something out of nothing.

Grabbing the throw from the back of the sofa, she lay down and tucked it up around her chin, staring at the dying embers of the fire. She felt caught in a familiar dream. Tommy was on the phone and he was trying to tell her where he was. She'd scribbled down the directions, but they'd be wrong, so she'd start, again and again and again, never getting it quite right.

Her heart would begin to race and her hands would sweat as she became more and more frantic. Finally, faced with her ineptitude, he'd hang up. She felt tears press at the corners of her eyes. Would she ever be able to let go of what had happened? Somehow, Tenley knew her guilt over her brother's death was holding her back. She couldn't change the past, but was she strong enough to change her future?

Alex had put his trust and faith in her abilities as an artist and a writer. He claimed she had a real talent. Tenley had heard those words a million times from her parents and from her grandparents, but she'd never believed them. They were merely trying to make her whole again.

But Alex was a stranger, someone who didn't know about her past. He could be objective. She pushed up on her elbow and stared at the crumpled paper scattered on the floor. She'd just have to try again.

"Tenley?"

She sat up and watched as Alex wandered through the kitchen and into the great room. "I'm here."

"What time is it? What are you doing up?"

"I was just working. Trying to figure out these new scenes for my story."

He stood in front of her, his naked body gleaming in the soft light from the fire. He ran his hand through his hair, then sighed. "Is everything all right?"

"Sure," she said. Tenley felt emotion well up in her throat, but she swallowed it back. "Everything is fine."

He sat down beside her, slipping his arm around her shoulders. "Sweetheart, don't worry about this. I don't expect you to finish it in one night. Or one month. You can take your time. I'll wait."

A tear slipped from the corner of her eye and she quickly brushed it away before he could see. But from his worried expression, Tenley could tell she hadn't been quick enough. "Sorry," she said, shaking her head. "I'm just exhausted."

"Talk to me."

"It's nothing. I'm just having a little meltdown. I'm tired and cranky and frustrated."

"Go ahead," he said. "You can melt in front of me if you want."

Another tear slipped from her eye, but this time she let it run down her cheek. "Really?"

He nodded, then pulled her closer. Tenley sobbed as the tears suddenly broke through her defenses. Nuzzling her face into his naked chest, she let them fall, the emotion draining out of her with each ragged breath.

For Alex's part, he simply sat beside her, smoothing his hand over her hair and whispering soft words against her temple. She clung to him as tightly as she could, as if his presence would somehow save her from her feelings. Then, slowly, the sadness dissolved, replaced by relief and resignation. She'd allowed her emotions to overwhelm her and she'd survived.

"Better?" he asked.

Tenley nodded. "God, I feel like such a dope. Look at this mess. I couldn't sleep and I just worked myself into a panic." She pressed her hand against his chest and looked up into his eyes. "I don't know why you like me. I'm a mess."

"You're not a mess," he said.

"I've made so many mistakes in my life, Alex. I let so much slip away. I should have listened to my parents. I should have gone to college. I should have studied art. Everything would have been different."

"But maybe not better," Alex said.

"What do you mean?"

"That story you wrote came from your life as it was, from the pain you felt at the time. If you'd done things differently, that story might never have come out."

She sniffled, brushing at her damp cheeks. "I don't know. I tried to be strong, but it was so much easier to just avoid thinking about it. I didn't want to make my parents happy, I didn't want to plan for my future. I just wanted to grieve. And I did, in the only way I knew how."

"That was the right thing for you to do, Tenley. You have to let these things take their natural course. You can't be something you aren't."

"My life should have begun when I graduated from high school or college. But it feels like it's beginning now. And that scares me. I'm twenty-six years old."

"It doesn't scare me. You can hold on to me as long as you need to."

"You're a really nice guy," she murmured, pressing a kiss to his chest. "Did anyone ever tell you that?"

"No. I think you're the first."

Tenley laughed. "Really?"

"You're the only one that matters," he said in a quiet voice. Alex took her hand and pressed a kiss to her palm. "Come on. Leave this for later and come back to bed."

Tenley shook her head. She'd only lie awake and stare at the ceiling until dawn. She needed something to occupy her mind. "I won't be able to sleep."

"I know what will relax you," he said. Alex stood and pulled her to her feet. "A nice, hot bath."

"You're going to give me a bath?"

"Well, I thought we'd give each other a bath. Then we'd go back to bed and sleep until we couldn't sleep anymore."

Intrigued by the suggestion, Tenley followed him to the bathroom and sat on the toilet seat as he filled the old claw-foot tub. She fetched her shampoo and soap from the shower stall and grabbed a washcloth from the rack on the wall.

When the tub was full, Alex undressed her, pulling her T-shirt off over her head and skimming her pajama bottoms to the floor. He held her hand as she stepped over the edge and slowly settled herself.

Then she leaned forward and held out her hand. "There's room for you, too."

Alex stepped in behind her, her body tucked neatly between his thighs. She leaned back against his chest and closed her eyes. "This is perfect."

"Yeah, it is," he said. "I need to get a bathtub at my apartment. A big one, just like this."

"Tell me about your place," she said.

"I live in a two-flat in Wicker Park," he said. "I have the second and third floor and I have tenants who live downstairs. It's an old house, built at the turn of the century. But I've renovated it inside. It's comfortable, but it's not as nice as this." He ran his hands through her hair. "This is like a home. It's warm and cozy. I like it here."

"When do you have to go back?" she asked.

"I was supposed to leave for a vacation in Mexico on Wednesday, but I missed my flight. I was planning to be gone through Monday, so I guess I'd have to leave Monday night?"

"That gives us four more days," she said.

"And three more nights," he said. "Doesn't seem like a long time, does it?"

"I'm sorry you had to miss your vacation," Tenley said.

"I'm not. This is the best vacation I've ever had."

She turned over, pressing her palms to his chest as she looked into his eyes. When she'd first met Alex, he'd been so charming, it had been difficult to believe anything he said. But now, as she lay in his arms, Tenley saw the real man beneath the charm, the sweet, considerate, affectionate guy that every girl wanted.

"I could fall asleep in this tub."

"Don't do that. You'd wake up all wrinkled." He scooped water into his hands and poured it over her hair, smoothing the damp strands away from her face. "There. I like you just like this."

"How is that?"

"With your hair out of your face, so I can see your

pretty blue eyes and your perfect nose." He bent closer and kissed her, tracing the shape of her mouth with his tongue. "And your lips."

"Do you realize that we've only known each other for just over three days?" Tenley asked.

"No, it's been longer than that," he said.

"Monday night. It's Friday morning."

He seemed stunned by the revelation. "That's... amazing." Alex drew in a sharp breath, then grabbed her hips. "Sit up. I'll wash your hair."

Tenley chuckled. "Slave boy has returned."

"Your wish is my command," he said, grabbing the bottle from the floor next to the tub. He tipped her head back and rubbed a small amount of the shampoo into her hair. "I think I need to get some of this. So when I'm back home, I can smell it and think of you."

It was difficult to imagine what her life would be like once he left. He'd changed everything for her. He'd carved out a place in her world and he fit perfectly. She had four days and three nights to prepare herself—to convince herself she could live without him.

It would be difficult to do when every moment they spent together seemed to be more perfect than the last. But Alex had taught her one thing. She was a lot stronger than she'd thought she was.

ALEX PUSHED OPEN the front door of The Coffee Bean and scanned the crowd inside, looking for Tenley's grandfather. He'd stopped by the gallery, only to find a note on the door indicating that Tom had gone to breakfast. Alex didn't know Sawyer Bay well, but he knew the best place for breakfast was The Coffee Bean.

Tom was sitting at a table with Harvey Willis, the two of them in deep discussion. Alex hesitated before he approached, knowing that the town police chief didn't have a high opinion of him.

"Morning," Alex said.

Harvey grinned. "Well, there he is. Were your ears burning? You've been the subject of some wild speculation 'round town."

"I'm sure I have," Alex replied.

Harvey got to his feet and indicated his empty chair. "Have a seat. It's all warmed up for you. Tom, nice talking to you. Thanks for the donation. Your pictures always bring a pretty penny in our raffle."

"Thanks, Harvey. I'll talk to you later."

Alex rested his hands on the back of the chair. "Mind if I sit?" he asked.

"Not at all. I've been expecting a visit from you. Would you like some coffee?" He twisted in his chair. "Audrey, bring us another cup of coffee, would you?"

The waitress nodded, then hurried over with a full pot and another menu. "What can I get you?"

Alex scanned the choices, then pointed to the Lumberjack Breakfast. It was what Tenley had ordered the last time they dined at The Coffee Bean. He was beginning to understand her point. After the previous night's activities in her bed, he was ravenous.

"So, I suppose you're here to discuss Tenley," Tom

said. "You're worried she might not want to go through with this?"

Alex shook his head. "No. She's agreed to the contract. We're going to publish her novel."

Tom grinned and clapped his hands. "I knew it. I knew something was going on with her."

"Going on?"

"Tenley has had a very hard time of it these past years. Lots of sadness in her life."

"Tell me about that," Alex said. "I know her brother died, that he drowned. And that it made her shut herself off to everyone around her. But that's all I know."

Tenley's grandfather took a slow slip of his coffee. "I'm not going to tell you anything. If Tenley wants you to know, she'll tell you. And if she does talk about it, then I think she's really ready to move on." He sighed. "If you feel a need to know, anyone in town can fill you in. Or you can read about it in the old newspapers at the library. May 15, 1999. That's when it happened." He paused. "But if I were you, I'd want to know her side of the story first. If she trusts you enough to tell you, then I think you might be the kind of man she needs in her life."

"I think I want to be that man," Alex said. "But I'm a little worried. I've gotten to know Tenley—her feelings can shift in the blink of an eye."

"Are you in love with her, Alex?"

He was surprised by the direct question. But then, it was clear where Tenley had gotten her plainspoken curiosity. "I don't know," he admitted. "I've never been in love before. I'm not quite sure how it's supposed to feel."

"I'd appreciate it if you'd be very careful with her heart. It was broken once and I'm not sure she'll be able to survive having it broken again."

"I won't hurt her," Alex said. "I can promise you that. But I can't guarantee she won't break my heart."

"She's a piece of work, isn't she?" Tom chuckled. "Oh, you should have seen the two of them. They were a pair. When they were born, their parents put them in separate cribs and they screamed until they were together again. After that, Tenley and Tommy were inseparable. When they started to talk, their words were gibberish to everybody else. They had their own language. No one understood it except the two of them." He reached into his back pocket and pulled out his wallet. "See. There they are. This was their tenth birthday."

Alex examined the photo. Tenley hadn't changed much. The dark hair and the pale blue eyes, the delicate limbs. "She was cute."

"After Tommy died, my son and his wife couldn't handle the grief. They grew apart, separated, and then decided to divorce. Tenley was uncontrollable, angry, lashing out at anyone who tried to get close. They ended up leaving, but she just flat-out refused. So she lived with her grandmother and me. I thought it was good she wanted to get back to her normal life, but that's not what happened. A few years later, I found out the reason she stayed was because she thought he might come back.

That the body they found wasn't really his and that he was alive."

"She's been waiting all this time?"

"She has. But I think she's stopped waiting for Tommy. I think maybe she's been waiting for you. Or someone like you. Someone she could trust. Someone who could give her the same confidence that her brother gave her. I think you've done that for her, Alex. And no matter what happens between the two of you, you need to respect that."

Alex had always shied away from commitment in the past, but this time, he wanted to make all the promises necessary to ensure Tenley's happiness. "I care about her. But if publishing this novel is going to hurt her in some way, I'll turn around and go back to Chicago today."

"No," Tom said. "I think you might be the best thing that's ever happened to her."

Alex smiled. "She's a very talented artist. And an incredible storyteller. I just want readers to see that."

"She and her brother used to draw cartoons all the time. After he died, she just stopped drawing. This is a big step for her. Don't do anything to mess it up, all right?"

"You can trust me," Alex said.

Tom's eyebrow arched up and he fixed Alex with a shrewd stare. "Can I? Will you stick with her, even when she's trying her damnedest to push you away? Because she will, you know. She'll find some excuse to run away and do everything to make you hate her."

"I think I can deal with that," he said, frowning. "I've used that technique myself on occasion." How many women had he charmed then ignored when he grew bored with the relationship? Except for the motivations, what Tenley did wasn't much different.

"You're taking on trouble," Tom warned. "But I'd venture to say the reward will be well worth the battle." He held up his coffee cup in a mock toast. "I wish you luck, young man."

They passed the rest of their time discussing Tenley's novel and what kind of opportunities publication would offer her. Alex was glad for Tom's insight into Tenley's behavior. Though there were moments when he thought he knew her well, he realized she was like a puzzle. Each individual piece was simple to understand, but it was how the pieces fit together that complicated matters.

When they were finished, Tom paid the bill, then invited Alex back to his studio, anxious to show him photos of Tenley's childhood. But Alex begged off. Tenley had closed herself in the studio at the house, determined to work on her new drawings. And Alex was anxious to see her progress.

But before he went back, he had to pick up his new phone from the Harbor Inn, call the office, then check out of his room at the bed-and-breakfast and move his things to Tenley's cabin. He and Tenley would spend the rest of his vacation together.

He walked back to the inn, where he'd parked the rental, then decided to surrender to his curiosity. He'd seen a sign on Main Street for the local library. It was past ten, so it would probably be open.

As he drove through the snow-covered streets, Alex wondered if it might be best just to let it go. Would it make a difference knowing the whole truth about Tenley's past? It might help him understand her insecurities a little better. And it could explain why it took her all these years to work through her grief.

He parked the SUV in an empty spot on the street and walked the short distance to the library, a small building that looked like it might have once been a bank. A young woman, not much older than Tenley, greeted him from the circulation desk.

"I'm interested in looking at some old newspapers," he said. "From this town, if possible. Back about ten years ago."

"That would be the Sawyer Bay Clarion," she said. "They stopped publishing it two years ago, but back issues can be found in the periodical section. If you want one from any further back than fifteen years, I'll have to go down to the basement and fetch them."

"Thanks," Alex said. He wandered to the back of the building and found the huge books on a shelf near a big library table. May 15th, 1999. He laid the book on the table and flipped through the yellowed pages. The paper was a weekly, so he found the article in the issue dated May 19th.

The headline was huge. LOCAL BOY DROWNS IN BOATING ACCIDENT. The words sent a shiver through him. Tenley had lived through this tragedy. As his gaze skimmed the story, he was stunned to learn that she'd nearly died as well. She'd been clinging to the overturned sailboat for four hours before she'd been found. Her brother hadn't been so lucky.

"It was a tragedy."

Alex glanced over his shoulder to find the librarian standing behind him. "I guess you found what you came for."

"Yes. Did you know them?"

"I went to high school with them both. They were a few grades younger than me, but everyone knows everyone in this town. I think it was the most tragic thing that ever happened in this community. Everyone loved them so much."

"I can't imagine what she went though. But why would they have gone out in bad weather?"

"They were always doing crazy things," she said. "Always getting in trouble. Some folks said it was bound to happen, one of them getting hurt. It's the way they were raised. No one ever said no. There was no discipline. Children need boundaries."

"She blames herself," he said.

"I heard she was the one who talked her brother into going outside the harbor. They were always challenging each other. Dares and double dares and triple dares. Everything was game to them." The librarian shook her head. "She never forgave herself. That's why she's... different."

He slammed the book closed. "I like different," Alex said in a cool tone. He nodded at the librarian and headed back toward the door. "And you can tell everyone in town, if they're wondering."

As he walked back to his SUV, he thought about what it must have been like for Tenley. He was close to his two sisters and couldn't imagine how he'd feel if anything ever happened to one of them. It would be like a part of his soul had been cut away. Not only had Tenley lost her twin brother, she'd probably blamed herself for the breakup of her parents' marriage.

Suddenly, the burden of her happiness seemed like too much to bear. What if he couldn't be the man she needed? What if he failed her in the end? This was all moving so fast. Alex wasn't sure he was ready for it to go any further.

Maybe he shouldn't have pried into the past. It might have been better to remain comfortably oblivious. He got behind the wheel, then turned the key in the ignition. Alex wasn't sure what the future held for the two of them. But if this was love, then he sure as hell was going to give it a chance.

"HAVE YOU SEEN Alex?" Tenley distractedly flipped through the mail, separating the envelopes into bills to be paid and checks to be cashed.

"I did," her grandfather said. "We had breakfast this morning at The Coffee Bean. Had a nice chat. Although I've never seen anyone eat as much for breakfast as he did. Except for you."

Tenley smiled. "I think I'm going to take him snowshoeing tonight. I love the woods after dark."

"Maybe he's over at the inn."

"He said he had to check in with his office. I hope nothing's wrong." She paused. "You don't think he had to go home, do you?"

"Without telling you? I don't think he'd do that."

"But what if there was an emergency? He could have tried calling me at home and I wasn't there."

"Then he would have called here. Or stopped before he left town. Don't worry, Tennie, he's not going to disappear."

The bell above the door rang and she smiled. "That's probably him. I'm just going to drop these at the post office and then I'm going. I promise I'll finish all this up next week."

"We're not exactly going crazy with customers these days," her grandfather said. "Maybe you should think about taking a week or two off. A trip to Chicago might be nice. There's a new impressionist exhibit at the Art Institute."

"I was going to drive into Green Bay. I'm thinking about enrolling in some classes this summer."

"I think that's a fine idea, Tennie. They've been trying to get me to come in and teach a class in acrylics. We could drive in together."

She gave her grandfather a quick kiss, then hurried out into the showroom, anxious to see Alex. But when she walked through the door, it was Randy who was waiting for her. Tenley stopped short. "What are you doing here?"

He gave her a sheepish shrug. "I came to apologize for the other night."

"You don't need to apologize."

"I do," Randy said. "And I'm sorry for being such a pest. But I've loved you for as long as I can remember. I've never said that to you and right now, I'm pretty sure it won't make any difference, but I had to say it."

"I'm sorry," Tenley said, shaking her head. "I don't feel the same way."

"And you may hate me for this, but I don't care." He held out a manila envelope. When she refused to take it, he set it on a nearby table. "I think you should know about this guy from Chicago. I did a little research on the Internet and he's not everything you think he is."

"Take it back," Tenley demanded, a defensive edge in her voice. "I don't need to see it." Cursing softly, she crossed the room and picked up the envelope, then shoved it at Randy. But he refused to touch it. Tenley ripped it in half and then in half again. "Go," she ordered. "Before I punch you in the nose again."

Randy slipped out the door and Tenley glanced down at the scraps in her hands. Her fingers were trembling and she wanted to scream. What right did he have to interfere in her life? People in this town spent too much time worrying about others. They ought to spend more time worrying about their own lives.

"Wasn't that Alex?"

Tenley spun around, her heart skipping a beat. "No."

"A customer."

"It was just Randy Schmitt. He wanted to drop something off for me." She held up the scraps. "It wasn't important." Tenley shoved the papers into her jacket pocket, then picked up the mail that she'd dropped on the floor. "I'll see you later. If Alex stops in, tell him I went home."

Tenley hurried out the door, anxious to leave all thoughts of her encounter with Randy behind. As she strode up the sidewalk to the post office, she passed several people she knew. They smiled and said hello and Tenley returned the greeting.

Usually people avoided her gaze, knowing she wouldn't respond. But things had changed over the past few days. Whatever they thought was going on between her and Alex suddenly made her "normal" again.

The odd thing was, she felt normal. She wanted to smile, even though she was still furious with Randy. In truth, lately, she found herself smiling for no reason at all. She picked up her pace as she walked and the next person she passed, Tenley made it a point to say hello first.

When she got to the post office, she made polite conversation with the postmaster and when she walked out, she held the door open for Mrs. Newton, the English teacher at the high school.

By the time she got back to her Jeep, parked beside the gallery, Tenley felt as if she'd accomplished something important. Though Sawyer Bay could be a difficult place to live, it also had its advantages.

She reached in her jacket pocket for her keys, but found the scraps of Randy's envelope instead. She pulled them out and searched for a trash can that wasn't covered with snow. In the end, she got in her car and set them on the seat beside her.

But her curiosity got the best of her. What had Randy found that warranted a personal visit and a plain manila envelope? All manner of possibilities came to mind. Alex Stamos was a criminal, a happily married man, a porn star.

Well, porn star wouldn't be that difficult to believe considering his prowess in bed. But criminals usually didn't run publishing companies. And she was pretty confident that Alex wasn't married. Maybe he'd been married in the past?

Though that really wouldn't change her feelings for him, she had to wonder why he wouldn't have mentioned it. She picked the papers out of the envelope and spread them out on the seat, piecing them together one by one.

They were pages printed off a Web site called SmoothOperators.com. From what Tenley could see, the pages were a file on Alex. Beneath each screen name was a paragraph describing Alex—most of them in very unflattering terms. As she read through them, Tenley realized that these were written by women Alex had dated—and dumped.

As she flipped through the pages, she was stunned at the sheer number of women who had something to say about him. He appeared to be a serial dater. He was known as "The Charmer," a nickname that appeared on the top of each page alongside his photo.

"'Modus operandi,'" she read. "'The Charmer finds more excitement in the chase than he does in what comes later. After he gets you into bed, it's bye-bye and onto the next girl. He can't seem to settle on just one mate because he feels compelled to make every woman fall in love with him. He'll love you and leave you, all in the same night.'"

This didn't seem like the Alex she knew. But then, did she really know him at all?

"'Stay away from this man,'" she read.

If this was Alex, and the picture proved it was, then perhaps she ought to be more careful. Maybe there wouldn't be a future for them after all. Tenley scanned the photos of the women next to the screen names. Every single one of them looked as if they'd stepped out of the pages of a fashion magazine. If they couldn't capture Alex's heart, what made her think she could?

She closed her eyes and leaned back into the seat. Who was she kidding? She and Alex had enjoyed a vacation fling, an affair that was meant to have a beginning and an end. When she'd found him, she'd been willing to settle for just one night. Now, she'd have almost an entire week.

It would have to be enough. After he left, she'd move on with her life. And if they saw each other again, they could enjoy a night or two in bed—no strings, no regrets. Tenley quickly picked up the scraps and shoved them into the glove compartment.

At least her relationship with Alex proved one thing. She was ready to fall in love. And someday, maybe she'd find a man like him, a man who made her feel like she could do anything and be anyone she wanted to be.

7

THE WOODS WERE SILENT around them. Alex held his breath, listening, waiting for some sound to pierce the night air. But there was nothing, just the dark sky and the bare trees and the moonlight glittering off the snow.

"Wow," he murmured. "In all my life, I'm not sure I've ever heard complete silence." He reached out and found her hand in the dark. "There's always some sort of noise in the city, even when it's quiet. It hums."

"Shh! Hear that?"

He listened and heard the flutter of wings behind them. "What is that?"

"Owl," she said. "Probably got a mouse. There are all kinds of things moving in the woods at night. In the summer, it's like a symphony of sound. But in the winter, the snow muffles everything."

He could barely see the features of her face in the moonlight, but he could hear the smile in her voice. "What if we get lost?" he said. "Will you protect me from the bears and the wolves?"

"We won't get lost. I know every inch of these woods. Every tree. I grew up here." She turned on the flashlight and began walking again, her snowshoes crunching against the snow. Alex followed her until she stopped at a large tree.

"See," she said, pointing to the trunk. Her gloved finger ran over an arrow carved into the tree, the head pointing down.

"Did you do that?"

Tenley nodded. "Underneath all this snow and about a foot or two of dirt is an old cigar tin. My brother and I buried a time capsule on our eighth birthday. We were going to dig it up when we turned eighteen."

"Did you? Dig it up?"

Tenley shook her head. "I didn't have the heart. I can't even remember what we put inside. Maybe this summer, I'll come here and find out."

"What was he like?"

"He was…like me. In every way. It was like we shared a brain. We knew what the other was thinking all the time. I could look at him and know the next words that were going to come out of his mouth. Some people say twins have a psychic connection. When I come out here sometimes, I can feel him. Does that sound crazy?"

"No," Alex said.

"I just wish I could go back and fix the mistakes I made."

"What mistakes?" Alex knew the answer to his question, but he wanted her to tell him. And to his surprise, she started talking. Maybe it was the fact that she couldn't see him in the dark or that they were out in the cold, alone.

"It was my idea to go out that night," she began. "I dared him to sail out to the island. He said no, but I wouldn't let it go. I kept picking at him and picking at him until he agreed."

"It's not your fault, Tenley. You were just a kid. You didn't know."

"I did. That's the point. I knew it was dangerous. So did he. But I wanted him to admire me. I wanted him to think I was the most important person in the world. I wanted proof that he loved me the best."

"But he did. You were important to him."

"I wasn't. Not anymore."

"I don't understand."

He heard her draw a ragged breath. "Tommy had a girlfriend. He told me all about her, how much he liked her. How he was going to ask her to go sailing with him that weekend. I knew she'd be afraid to go outside the harbor. But I wasn't afraid. I had to prove to him that I was better than she was."

Alex reached out for her, but she pulled away, stepping back into the darkness. "Tenley, what happened was an accident. You didn't cause it. There's a million and one ways that bad things can happen. A million and one reasons why they do. You didn't create the bad weather, the cold water or the wave that turned over the boat."

"We were out there because of me," she said, bitterness suffusing her tone. "Because I was jealous of some silly girl with blond hair and pretty clothes."

He saw the tears streaming down her face, glittering in the moonlight. Alex wanted to take her into his arms and make everything better. But he knew how much it had cost her to tell him. By trying to brush it away, he would only trivialize her feelings. "What if you had been the one to die that night? What if Tommy had lived? And he'd tortured himself the same way you've been doing? How would you have felt about that?"

"Angry," she said. "But I wouldn't blame him. He'd never do anything to deliberately hurt me."

"Don't you think he knew that about you? Don't you think he realized how much you loved him? He wouldn't want you to spend the rest of your life mourning his death. Hell, I don't know Tommy. But if he was anything like you, he'd tell you to stop acting like such a baby and get on with your life."

Tenley sat down in the snow. "I feel like I'm ready to let it go. But I'm afraid if I do, I'll forget him. And then I won't have anyone."

He squatted down in front of her, reaching out to cup her face in his gloved hands. "You'll have me," Alex said.

"No, I won't. You're leaving in a few days."

"I don't live that far away, Tenley."

"Don't," she murmured, brushing his hands away. "Don't make any promises you can't keep. I'm fine with what we've had. I don't need anything more."

This was it, Alex thought. Her grandfather had warned him it was coming, but he hadn't expected her to turn on him for no reason—and so soon. "What if I do? Need more, I mean."

"I'm sure you'll find plenty of girls eager to take care of your needs."

"Do you think that's what this is about? Sex?"

She stumbled to her feet and brushed the snow off her backside. Then she shone the flashlight in his face. "That's all this was *ever* about. We enjoy each other in bed. There's nothing to be ashamed of."

"I don't believe you," Alex said. "I refuse to believe you don't feel something more."

"What I feel doesn't make a difference. Come on, Alex, be reasonable. We can pretend that we'll see each other again, we might even make plans. But once we're apart, the desire is bound to fade. I can deal with that. Don't worry, I'm not going to fall apart on you."

Alex felt a surge of anger inside of him. She sounded so indifferent, but he knew it was a lie. He had seen it in her eyes, had felt it in the way she touched him. They shared a connection that couldn't be broken with just a few words and a wave goodbye.

"We should go back," she muttered. "I'm getting cold."

He knew what would happen when they returned to the cabin. Tenley would find a way to smooth over their discussion and she'd lure him into bed. And once again, he'd be left certain he was falling in love with her, yet completely unsure of her feelings for him.

Alex had to wonder if he'd ever know how she truly felt. Would she ever be brave enough to admit that she needed him? Or that she wanted someone to share her life? Maybe Tenley was right. Maybe they both ought to just move on.

She pointed the flashlight out in front of them and

retraced their steps in the snow. Alex had no choice but to follow her. They walked for a long while in silence, but when he saw the lights from the yard, Alex suddenly regretted giving up his room at the inn.

He wasn't angry with her. He knew why Tenley was pushing him away. But Alex wondered if she could ever fully trust him. Or trust any man. He found it odd that her insecurities didn't come from a series of bad relationships, but from never having experienced a relationship at all.

She'd obviously had sex before. She was far too comfortable in bed. But he suspected she treated sex the same way she treated a hike or a ride in her sleigh—a pleasant activity to pass the time and nothing more. Truth be told, that was the way he'd always approached it as well—until he'd met her.

From the moment he'd first touched her, Alex felt something powerful between them. And sex became more than just physical release—it became a way to communicate his feelings for her. For the first time in his life, he was actually making love.

"I think I'm going to work for a while," Tenley said. "I'll be in later. Don't wait up."

"Fine," he said.

They parted ways on the porch, Alex watching as she walked toward the barn. He ought to pack his bags and leave. Let her see how much she liked her life without him in it. Maybe, with some time apart, she'd actually realize what they'd shared was special.

He unbuckled his snowshoes, then stepped inside to

find the dogs waiting. "Go ahead," he said, moving aside. They bounded out into the snow in a flurry of flying feet and wagging tails. He watched them play. Dog and Pup.

She hadn't even bothered to name her dogs. Was she afraid they were going to leave her, too, someday? He wasn't sure what the two cats were named, if they even had names. And as far as she was concerned, he was probably just…Guy or Dude.

Alex had cast aside more women than he cared to count. Why couldn't he bring himself to do the same with Tenley? Instead of being apathetic, he found himself angry. He'd made a difference in her life and she refused to acknowledge it. They were better people together than they were apart.

He saw the light go on in the tower studio and stepped into the shadows of the porch. Tenley appeared in the window overlooking the cabin. He watched as she moved about, remembering the previous afternoon and how she'd talked him out of his clothes.

Alex shook his head, wondering how this would all end. Hell, he couldn't believe it had begun in the first place. Had he not ended up in that snowdrift, none of this would have happened. Eventually, he would have tracked down Tenley, made his proposal and been on his way. On any other day, he might have looked right past her, unaware of the incredible woman she was.

But something had brought them together, some great karmic design, some strange twist of fate. And he had to believe that same force would keep them together, even though she was doing her damnedest to drive them apart.

"IT'S BETTER THIS WAY," Tenley murmured to herself. She paced back and forth across the width of the studio, her nerves on edge, her mind spinning endlessly. She wasn't supposed to fall in love. She'd never meant for it to happen. But now that it had, Tenley needed to find a way to stop herself.

Though she'd heard of people who'd fallen in love at first sight, Tenley never believed it was possible. Lust at first sight, maybe. But love took time to grow. How could you possibly love someone you didn't know?

"That's right," she muttered. "You can't love Alex. You don't even know him."

She pressed her hand to her heart. It wasn't love. But it sure felt like something she'd never experienced before. And she'd never been in love in her life.

Tenley stopped in front of the table and picked up the new drawing she'd done for the second chapter. It was as close to perfect as she could make it and it was good. Even she was proud of the effort, and Tenley was her own worst critic.

The fact that she was able to believe in herself as an artist was Alex's doing. She owed him a huge debt of gratitude. But did she owe him her heart? It seemed to be the only thing he wanted from her. Tenley's heart was a mangled mess, shattered in a million pieces and stuck back together again with duct tape and school paste and chewing gum.

Who would want a heart like that, a heart so close to breaking again? A heart that wasn't strong enough to love. Tenley sat down in her chair and cupped her chin in her hand. Slowly, she flipped through her story.

And it was her story. Cyd was everything she'd wanted to be—strong, determined, blessed with powers that could alter the past. But as she looked at the pictures she'd drawn, Tenley saw that Cyd was just ink on paper. Every move she made was part of an intricate plot planned out ahead of time. She had all the answers.

Real life was a different matter. Tenley had no control over the plot. There was no plan. Nothing was black and white. Instead, she was left to navigate through a world filled with shades of gray.

Did she love Alex or didn't she? The answer wasn't that simple. Perhaps she had the potential to love him. Maybe there was a tiny part of her that loved him already. But if asked for a yes or no answer, Tenley couldn't give one.

She shoved the papers back and stood, the walls of the studio closing in around her. Grabbing her coat, Tenley ran down the stairs and out into the cold night. She wrapped her arms around herself and tipped her head up to the sky, staring at the stars.

What came next in her story? Would she let it unfold in front of her? Or would she try to manipulate the plot? Though it might be nice to possess a superpower or two, Tenley suspected there was no power in the world that could make Alex love her if he didn't want to. She had to be prepared to let him go and to do it without any regrets.

The snow crunched beneath her boots as she walked back to the cabin. The great room was lit only by the fading fire and the light from above the kitchen sink. Pup and Dog came out to greet her and she gave them both a pat on the head. Tenley tiptoed down the hall and peeked into her bedroom. A stab of disappointment pierced her heart when she saw Alex wasn't waiting in her bed.

The door to the guest room was closed and she could only assume he was sending her a signal. She wasn't welcome. Tenley walked back to the kitchen, her wet boots squeaking on the wood plank floor. She kicked them off at the door and shrugged out of her jacket, tossing it over the back of the sofa.

A survey of the refrigerator yielded nothing interesting to eat, but she felt compelled to munch in an effort to take her mind off the man sleeping in her guest room. They'd spent the past four nights in each other's arms. It didn't seem right, sleeping all alone.

Tenley grabbed an apple from the basket on the counter, then walked back to her bedroom. She took a huge bite, then tossed the apple on the bed and began to remove her clothes. But in the end, exhaustion overwhelmed her and she flopped down, face-first on the sheets, still half-dressed. She found the apple and took another bite, then carefully considered her options.

She could do the sensible thing, crawl beneath the covers of her own bed, close her eyes and pray she'd fall asleep before giving in to her impulses. Or she could do the reckless thing and strip off all her clothes, walk into the guest room and get into bed with Alex. Or she could lie here and think of other options.

The cats were curled up on her pillow and she rolled over and pressed her face into Kittie's fur. Kattie opened her eyes and watched Tenley for a moment, then nuzzled her face into her paws and went back to sleep. This was what she'd be reduced to after Alex left— searching for affection from her pets.

She'd survived on their love before he'd walked into her life. So why did the prospect seem so unsatisfying now? "I love you," she murmured to the cats. "I do." But they didn't open their eyes. "I know you love me. You don't have to say the words. I can tell by the way you're lying there that you love me." She paused. "God, am I pathetic."

With that, Tenley sat up and raked her hands through her hair. Then she grabbed a book from the pile on her bedside table. But as she flipped through the pages, one by one, she couldn't find anything that might occupy her mind. She could bake some cookies. Or clean the fireplace. Or scrub the bathroom floor. Tenley drew a deep breath. Or she could walk into Alex's room and do what she really wanted to do—make love to him for the rest of the night.

She crawled out of bed and tiptoed to his door, then slowly opened it, wincing at the squeaky hinges. The room was dark, the only light coming from the hall. Tenley stood next to his bed, then silently knelt down beside it, her gaze searching his face.

There were times when his beauty took her breath

away. Men weren't supposed to be beautiful, but she could look at Alex with an artist's eye and see the perfection of his long limbs and muscled torso. This was the kind of man the Greeks sculpted in ancient times, the epitome of the human form, from his well-shaped hands to his lovely feet.

She thought back to the sketches she'd made of Alex. For the first time in her life, she'd felt like an artist. And she'd understood the need for a muse. Drawing Alex brought out her passion for her art. When she looked at his naked body, everything she saw through her eyes came out on the sketchpad.

Her fingers clenched and she longed for a pencil and pad, wanting to capture this scene in front of her. The frustration she felt earlier was gone and now she felt nothing but regret for her sharp words. He didn't deserve them. Alex had been nothing but kind and encouraging. No matter what those other women claimed, he'd been a perfect gentleman.

Tenley didn't know how much longer this would last. She suspected the feelings might fade once he returned to Chicago. But they still had three more days together. The least she could do was put aside her insecurities and make their moments together count for something.

Holding her breath, Tenley crawled into bed beside him, still dressed in her jeans and long-sleeved T-shirt. She felt him move behind her and then his arms circled around her waist and he pulled her against his body. His soft sigh tickled the back of her neck and a moment later, he pressed his lips to the same spot.

Tenley smiled, holding on to his hands and allowing her body to relax. He didn't need to say a word. Just his touch was enough to know that she'd been forgiven. And though Tenley wanted to strip off her clothes and make love to him, there was something wonderful about just being in his arms, lying next to him in his bed.

They had three more days and two more nights. There would be plenty of time to reignite the passion between them. She closed her eyes and waited for sleep to take the last of her tensions from her body.

But the noise in her head refused to quiet. Tenley drew a deep breath and then let it out slowly, before turning in Alex's embrace. Facing him, she smoothed her hands over his features, memorizing the feel of them in the dark.

When he brushed his mouth against hers, Tenley realized he was awake. She touched her lips to his and slowly the kiss grew deeper and more passionate. But there was an edge of desperation to each caress they shared, as if they both knew that the clock was ticking down on their time together.

With each soft sigh and each whispered word, Tenley grew more frantic to feel him inside her. When he began to undress her, she impatiently tore off her shirt and kicked out of her jeans. Once she was naked, Alex pulled her beneath the sheets, into the warmth of his body.

He was already hard and as he moved against her, his shaft pressed into the soft flesh of her abdomen. This was all she needed in life, this wonderful warm feeling of anticipation. Alex could smooth his hands over her skin and she'd lose herself in a wave of sensation.

There was more at work here than just physical attraction. She ached for that moment when she felt most vulnerable, when their souls seemed exposed. At that instant, the past melted away and Tenley felt alive and aware. Though she'd had men in her bed, not one of them had ever made her feel a fraction of what Alex did.

She reached for the box of condoms on the bedside table, surprised to find just one left inside. He smiled as she smoothed it over the length of his shaft, his breath coming in soft, short gasps.

He rolled her beneath him, then pulled her leg up alongside his hip. Probing gently, he found her entrance and in one sure motion, he slipped inside of her. Tenley groaned at the thrill that raced through her body.

There was nothing in the world that had ever felt this good. And Tenley knew this was what it was like to want a man so much her body ached for his touch and her soul cried out for his love. If this was all she had in the world, she could be happy forever.

But happiness didn't always last. It could be snatched away in the blink of an eye. At least she knew when the end would come. And she'd be prepared.

THE RINGING WOKE Alex up from a deep sleep. He opened one eye, searching for the source. It wasn't his watch. That was still in the refrigerator.

"What is that?" Tenley murmured, turning her face into the pillow. "Turn it off."

"I can't find it. Where's the clock?"

"It's not an alarm clock. I don't have an alarm clock."

Alex sat up and searched the room, then noticed the sound was coming from his pants, which were tossed over a nearby chair. He stumbled out of bed and picked them up, then found the new BlackBerry in his pocket. He pushed the button and put it to his ear.

"What?"

"It's Tess. I'm sorry to call you so early but we have a huge problem. The new press just went down and we're in the middle of the Marberry project. It's Saturday and none of the techs are answering their phones. We're supposed to deliver this job on Monday and we've still got to run it through bindery. I need you to come home."

"Aw, hell." Alex rubbed his face with his hand, trying to clear the sleep from his brain. "It's going to take me a while. I can probably make some calls from the road. I'm going to call Marberry first and see if we can't push back delivery. How much of a hit can we take on our price?"

"Five percent at the most. But don't offer him a discount on this job. Tell him we'll discount the next one. At least we know we'll get him back as a customer, then."

"Do you have to talk so loud?" Tenley groaned. Alex sat down on the edge of the bed and put his pillow over her head.

"Who is that?" Tess asked. "Oh, my God. Are you with a woman? Good grief, Alex, send her home, get in your car and point it toward Chicago. I'll see you in…five hours."

"I've got to pick up my car from the garage and they won't open until eight or nine. It'll take me at least six hours to get back, so schedule a meeting with the production team at three. We'll get this sorted out."

Tess hung up and Alex flopped back down on the bed, the phone still clutched in his hand "I have to go," he said.

Tenley pushed up on her elbows, her hair sticking up in unruly spikes. "Go where?"

"Back to Chicago. We've got an emergency with one of our presses at the Elgin plant."

"No," Tenley moaned. "You're supposed to stay until Monday."

Alex rolled over and drew her into his embrace. "I know. Maybe I can come back. I'll take care of business and if everything's all right, I can drive back late tonight. I could be back here by midnight."

She closed her eyes and for a long time didn't speak. Alex thought she'd fallen asleep again. But then, she opened her eyes. "You have to go," she said. "We only had a few days left anyway. It's all right."

"No, I'll come back," Alex insisted.

Tenley shook her head, then pressed her finger to his lips. "No. It's better this way. You need to get back to work. And I need to work on the novel. I can't do that with you here."

"How about next weekend? I could drive up on Friday night." All Alex needed was a promise that there would be a next time. He didn't want to leave without knowing exactly where they stood.

Tenley reached out and smoothed her hand over his cheek. "Alex, we both knew, going in, how difficult this would be. You're down there and I'm here. Throw in the whole business thing and it gets too complicated. I'd like to believe we're both smart enough to see that and save ourselves the pain of trying to make a relationship work."

Alex couldn't believe what he was hearing. He'd never been dumped in his life and this sounded suspiciously like the big heave-ho. He brushed the hair out of her eyes and turned her face up to his. But all he saw in her eyes was complete honesty. Had he misread the depth of her feelings for him?

"So this is it?" he asked.

"I know you've done this before," Tenley said with a small smile. "A guy like you doesn't stay single for as long as you have without breaking a few hearts. It's easy."

"This doesn't seem easy to me," he said.

"It will get better." She leaned forward and brushed a kiss across his lips. "At least I didn't break your heart and you didn't break mine. I think we both got out of this feeling pretty good."

She was right. Still, he wanted her to want him to stay, so much that she would grasp at any chance to see him again. That was what women did. They got all crazy and clingy and demanding. But then, Tenley hadn't ever acted like the women he'd dated. So it would make sense she'd just cut him loose without a second thought.

"You're sure about this?"

"Absolutely sure," she said.

He frowned. "So, I guess we'll be talking to each other about the novel. You'll work on the changes. And when they're done, we'll discuss them."

"Yes. If I have any questions, I'll call you."

Alex sat up and swung his legs off the bed. Then he ran his hands through his hair. This just didn't seem right—hell, it didn't *feel* right. Every instinct in his body told him not to leave her like this, to make it clear he wanted more than what they'd already shared.

She slipped her arms around him from behind and rested her chin on his shoulder. "I am going to miss you. I like having you here when I wake up."

"That's a good reason to see each other again, isn't it?"

She crawled out of bed and pulled him to his feet. "Come on. Get dressed. I'll make you something to eat while you pack. And I'll call the garage and tell them you're coming for your car."

Tenley grabbed her T-shirt from the floor and tugged it over her head. "Wait a second," Alex said. "Not so fast." He pulled her against his body and kissed her, smoothing his hands up beneath her shirt until he found the soft flesh of her breasts.

Tenley giggled. "Wanted to cop one last feel?"

"Hey, I'm a guy. I have to have something to think about on the ride home."

Tenley dragged her T-shirt back over her head and threw it on the bed. "All right. I'll cook breakfast in the nude. That should give you plenty to think about for the next two or three days." She gave him a devilish smile, then walked out of the bedroom, a tantalizing sway to her hips.

Alex poked his head out the door and watched her as she moved down the hallway. Tenley had the most incredible body. And she didn't even work at it.

He gathered the clothes he'd left in Tenley's room and took them back into the guest room, then dug through his duffel for something comfortable to wear. He found a clean T-shirt, pulled it over his head, then stepped into his last pair of clean boxers. His missing jeans were mixed in with Tenley's laundry and he tugged them on, then searched for his socks.

"Scrambled or fried?" she called from the kitchen.

"Just toast," Alex called. "And coffee. Really black." He might as well get back to his regular routine as soon as possible. Besides, he wouldn't be spending the day and night with Tenley, so there wasn't much need for extra energy.

When he got out to the kitchen, he found Tenley standing at the counter, sipping a cup of coffee, still completely naked. She handed him a mug and then retrieved his toast from the toaster.

"I like this," he said, letting his gaze drift down the length of her body. "If a guy had this every day, he'd never get to work in the morning."

"It's a lot better in the summer," Tenley said. "I'm freezing."

Alex gathered her up in his arms and pressed a kiss to the top of her head. "You are, by far, the most interesting woman I've ever met, Tenley Marshall. I'm not going to forget you, even if you do make breakfast with your clothes on. Go get dressed."

She ran back to her bedroom and reappeared a minute later in flannel pajamas and slippers. She sat down next to him at the end of the island, sipping her coffee and waiting for him to finish his toast.

"I did have a wonderful time," she said with a warm smile. "I'm glad I stopped and rescued you."

"I'm glad you did, too." He reached out and slipped his hand through the hair at her nape. Gently, Alex pulled her forward until their lips met. He knew it might be the last time he kissed her, so he tried to make it as sweet and perfect as possible. When he finally drew back, Alex looked down, taking in all the small details of her face, committing them to memory.

There was a time when he thought her odd, but now, Alex was certain she was someone so special, so unique that he might never meet another woman like her again. He drew a steadying breath, then stood. The longer he waited, the more difficult this was going to be.

"I have to go. Now. Or I'm never going to leave."

Tenley nodded. "All right." She hugged him hard, then pushed up on her toes and gave him a quick kiss. "I'll see you, Alex."

He wanted to gather her in his arms and show her what a real goodbye kiss should be. But in the end, Alex took one last look, smiled and turned for the door. "I'll see you, Tenley."

The trek out to his rental car was the longest walk of his life. Every step required enormous willpower. When he looked back, she was standing on the porch in her pajamas, the cold morning wind blowing at her dark hair. He waved as he drove past the house to the driveway. And all the way to town, Alex tried to come up with an excuse to send him back to the cabin.

Tenley was right. They'd been caught up in a wildly enjoyable affair, but that was all it had been. Passion had turned to infatuation and he'd mistaken it for love. Love didn't happen in four days or even four weeks. And though his interest in other women had always faded quickly, Alex knew that his feelings for Tenley would be with him for a very long time. He would never, ever forget Tenley Marshall.

"YOUR PERSPECTIVE is off here."

Tenley studied the drawing, then nodded. "You're right. I always make that mistake." She cursed softly. "This is why I should have gone to art school. People will see things like that and know I'm an amateur."

"No, they won't. This is highly stylized, Tenley. You can break a lot of rules. In fact, in this kind of work, you can make up your own rules. It's your universe. I'm just pointing out some areas you might want to consider," her grandfather said.

"Right," she murmured.

It had been three days since Alex had walked out of her life. He'd called twice, but she'd ignored his calls, knowing it would be easier if they didn't speak for a while. Still, she'd listened to the sound of his voice on her voice mail over and over again.

She'd been working on the novel nonstop, but her progress had been cursed with fits and starts. With only her own resources to depend upon, Tenley found herself second-guessing the decisions she made. Her first impulse was to call Alex and discuss her concerns with him. But she realized that if she wanted to be an artist, she'd have to stand on her own. Or fail.

Though failing had once been a viable option, the more time she spent on the novel, the more Tenley wanted to make it work. This was a great story, a story that was so tightly woven into her own that she had trouble separating herself from Cyd. She'd grown to like the girl. She was strong and resourceful and determined. She was a survivor.

Yet even with a new story swirling around in her head, Tenley still couldn't keep her thoughts from wandering to Alex. She hadn't thought it would be this difficult. Once he was gone, she assumed her life would get back to normal. Sure, she'd think about him occasionally, but thoughts of him would soon fade.

In reality, she'd become obsessed with remembering. Each night, before she fell asleep, she'd go through each image in her head, lingering over them like a photo album. Yesterday, she'd actually made a drawing of Alex in the perfect state of arousal and she was quite taken with it, until she realized it was bordering on pornography.

On the floor in front of the fire, in the sauna, in the

studio, in his room—everywhere she turned there were reminders of him.

"Tenley!"

"What?" She stood up, spinning around to find her grandfather standing behind her, his arms crossed over his chest.

"How long are you going to be like this?"

"Like what?"

"Your young man has been gone for, what, three days?"

"Yes, three days."

"And when is he coming back?"

"He's not. And he's not my young man. He's just a guy I knew for a while."

"I see. And how long do you plan to mope around?"

"I'm not moping. I'm just distracted. I have a lot of things on my mind and not enough time to think about them all. Speaking of which, if you don't go through those bills of sale and mark the inventory numbers on them, I'm going to have a lot more to be crabby about than Alex Stamos."

"This arrived for you today." Her grandfather held up a large envelope. The logo for the university in Green Bay was emblazoned on the corner.

Tenley took it from his hand. "Thanks."

"So you're going to start school?"

"Yes," she said firmly. "This summer. I'm going to take a writing class, too."

"Why not spread your wings a little further, Tennie? Check out some other schools. The Art Institute in

Chicago has a great school. You could go down there and stay for the summer, really immerse yourself in something new."

Though the Art Institute might have a fabulous school, Tenley knew why her grandfather was pushing that choice. It would give her the opportunity to rekindle her relationship with Alex. The thought had crossed her mind more than once. But she wanted to simplify her life, not make it more complicated. "I can't do that. I have responsibilities here. I have my dogs and cats and horses to care for. And I don't have the money to stay in Chicago for the summer. If I go to Green Bay, I can drive back and forth."

"I'll give you the money," her grandfather said.

"No, you won't. You don't have the money to give me."

"No?" He laughed. "I have a lot of money. Money you don't even know I have. I've put it all in a trust for you. I don't think you should have to wait for me to kick the bucket before you can use it. So I'm going to give it to you now."

"I can't take your money," Tenley said. "You should spend it on yourself."

"I intend to. In fact, now that you're planning on attending school, I might just go somewhere warm for the winter."

"You hate California," she said.

"I was thinking about Greece."

Tenley gasped. "Greece? Since when?"

He picked up a paintbrush and examined it closely.

"I've always wanted to go to Greece. Your grandmother hated to fly, so we couldn't go. And after she died, I had you to watch out for. But now that you're moving on, I think I should do the same."

Emotion welled up inside of her. She'd never meant to be a burden on her grandfather. She was supposed to care for him, not the other way around. "I'm sorry. I didn't realize that you— You should go. Oh, it would be wonderful. Think of all the things you could paint." With a sob, she threw her arms around her grandfather's neck. "Thank you for being so patient with me. I'm sorry it took me so long to figure things out."

He patted her back. "Not to worry. It all worked out in the end. You found a man and that's the only thing that matters."

"I didn't find a man," Tenley said stubbornly. "Alex went back to Chicago. He's gone."

"What difference does that make? If he's the one you want, then a few hundred miles won't matter. When I met your grandmother, she was living in the Upper Peninsula. and I was living in Minot, North Dakota. We managed to find a way to make it work."

"I don't want to make it work," Tenley said. "I'm not ready to be in love."

Her grandfather shook his head and chuckled. "It's not like you can prepare for it. It just happens and when it does, you have to grab it and hang on for dear life. It doesn't come along that often."

Tenley took her drawings and put them back inside her portfolio, then zipped it up. "Well, I don't want to be in love. Not right now. I have too many other things I have to do. It would just get in the way."

He reached out and placed his hand over hers. "Tennie, I really don't think you have a whole lot of control over that. Don't get me wrong, I've always admired your resolve. But on this one you're wrong." He tapped her portfolio. "Good work. When you're done, I think a trip to Chicago might be in order. It'll give you a chance to check out the school at the Art Institute."

"What would you do without me during the summer?"

"I was thinking I'd hire one of those college students who are always wanting to intern at the gallery. Someone who's not so much trouble."

Tenley giggled. "You're not going to get rid of me with insults." She picked up her portfolio and walked to the door. "If I go to Chicago for the summer, you'd have to take care of my dogs and cats. They'd have to move in with you. And we'd have to board the horses."

He held out his hands. "A small price to pay for your happiness."

She zipped up her coat and walked out the door into the chilly afternoon sun. Once, her days had been spent in a holding pattern, just waiting for something to push her forward again. Alex had done that for her. He'd given her a reason to move on and for that, she'd be forever grateful.

Someday, she'd tell him that. Someday in the distant future—when she'd be able to look at him and not wonder if she'd given up too soon.

8

TENLEY HAD BEEN to the Art Institute several times when she was younger. As she walked down the front steps, looking back at the classic facade, she let the memories wash over her. Her parents had been together and Tommy was still alive. They'd rushed up the front steps, racing each other to the door, hoping to see everything in just one day. And while her mother and father lingered over the paintings, she and Tommy found their favorite spots.

Tenley had been fascinated by the miniatures, like little dollhouses with each tiny piece of furniture perfectly reproduced. Tommy was drawn to the Greek and Roman coins, comparing them to his collection of Indian head pennies at home.

It had been one of the last times they'd traveled together as a family. But to her surprise, the memory didn't cause the usual ache in her heart. Instead, she felt only a tiny bit of melancholy as she recalled the affection they'd all had for each other. Tommy had lived a short life, but he had been well loved.

Maybe that was what life was all about—searching

for a place to feel accepted. Since Alex had left, Tenley had made the decision to walk away from the past and begin again. Though she was excited at the prospect, she was also a bit frightened.

She'd spent the afternoon strolling through galleries, studying the artists and wondering if they'd ever had the same doubts she was having. To pacify her grandfather, Tenley had met with an admissions specialist for the Art Institute school and, in the end, decided to apply for a three-week session in June and another in August. Six weeks away from home during her grandfather's busiest season would be difficult, but he'd assured her he could get along with temporary help.

Housing was offered by the school, but it didn't allow for pets. So Dog and Pup and her two cats were going to have to live at her grandfather's place while she was gone. Josh could take care of the horses, moving them over to his family's farm to make it more convenient, and she'd drive home on the weekends to make sure everything was running smoothly.

Yet, even though she tried to focus on the business at hand, her thoughts constantly shifted to the real reason she'd come to Chicago—Alex. They'd spoken several times since he'd left, mostly about the novel. But sometimes they drifted into conversation about their time together.

Though neither one of them wanted to make the first move to rekindle their romantic relationship, there always seemed to be a tension simmering right below the surface—as if the thoughts were there, waiting to be expressed.

Tenley stepped to the curb and held up her hand to hail a cab. A few seconds later, a taxi pulled up and she got inside. She reached into the pocket of her portfolio for Alex's business card and gave the cabbie the address.

Though she'd come to Chicago to see Alex, her excuse for the trip was a meeting she'd scheduled with her editor. She'd finished the requested revisions and had completed the new artwork for the changes. Rather than sending them via courier, Tenley had decided to deliver them personally.

Marianne Johnson, her editor, felt it important they meet, but Tenley was really hoping to take a few moments to say hello to Alex. It had been nearly three weeks since he'd left and even though she thought of him every hour of every day, she was beginning to forget the tiny details that had fascinated her so. The closest thing she had to a photograph was the picture from the Smooth Operators Web site. And then she had her drawings, but none of those had a face with the body.

All she needed was a few seconds to recharge her memory. As the cab wove through the late-afternoon traffic, Tenley tried to imagine how it would be. She'd stand at his door and say a quick hello. He'd ask her to come in and sit down, but she'd beg off, explaining that she had a meeting scheduled with her editor. He'd ask her to dinner and she'd tell him she was driving back that night. He'd say the traffic was bad until later and she ought to wait.

All she really wanted to know was that she and Alex could deal with each other as business associates. The past was the past. It might not have been so important before, but in the past few weeks, Tenley had begun to imagine building a career as a graphic novelist. She'd already come up with four or five new ideas for stories.

The headquarters for Stamos Publishing was located in the South Loop in a huge brick building that had been modernized with new windows and a gleaming entrance. One corner was constructed entirely of glass, revealing a printing press in full operation.

Tenley paid the cabbie, then hopped out of the car, clutching her portfolio to her chest. She'd left her Jeep parked in the lot at the hotel, her bags in the trunk, preferring to let someone else do the driving while she was in town. Later tonight, she'd pick it up and head home.

She checked in at the front desk and was given a badge to clip onto her pocket. A few seconds later, Marianne Johnson burst through the door, a wide smile on her face. "Tenley! Gosh, it's a pleasure to finally meet you." She held out her hand. "How was your drive down? The weather looked good."

"I actually came down yesterday afternoon. I went to the Art Institute this morning and spent most of the day there."

"Wonderful! First, I want to take you by Alex's office. I know he's in and I'm sure he wants to say hello."

"Oh, I don't want to bother him," Tenley said, suddenly succumbing to an attack of nerves. What if he wasn't thrilled to see her? What if they had nothing to say to each other? She'd built this meeting up in her mind for three weeks, ever since Alex had left Door County. And now that it was here, she wanted to run back home.

"It's no bother. When I told him you were coming, he insisted we stop by. Come on."

They wove through a warren of hallways, past small offices and large conference areas, all occupied by production personnel. Marianne took her back to the pressroom and explained to her that her novel would be printed at their new plant in Elgin and that she would be invited to do a press check once the process had begun.

By the time they stepped inside the elevator, Tenley's heart was slamming in her chest and she could barely breathe. What if she couldn't speak? What if everything she said sounded stilted and contrived?

"Our sales and marketing offices are up here," Marianne said, after they arrived at the second floor. "We're so excited about publishing your novel. I think this new imprint is going to be the best thing that's ever happened to this company."

Unlike the production offices, the second floor was quiet, the hum of the printing presses barely audible. Marianne took her through a set of glass doors, then smiled at the receptionist. "Alex wanted us to stop in," she explained.

Tenley took a deep breath. She'd brought a new outfit for the occasion. She wore a hand-woven jacket with a bright chartreuse turtleneck, a short black skirt and leggings underneath. Lace-up ankle boots and a studded belt finished off the ensemble. In her opinion, it was edgy and cool and it made her look like a real artist.

"Alex? I've got Tenley here."

Marianne stepped aside and directed her through a wide doorway. Tenley pasted a smile on her face and walked in. The moment their eyes met, she felt as if she'd been hit in the chest with a brick. Her heart fluttered and her breathing grew shallow and she felt a bit light-headed. "Hello." It was all she could manage.

"Hello, Tenley. Come on in. Sit down."

His voice was warm and deep and caused a shiver to race through her body. "Oh, I can't stay. Marianne and I have a meeting. And then I have to get back on the road. I've got a long drive home tonight. I just wanted to say hi." She gave him a little wave and a weak laugh. The words had just tumbled out of her mouth so fast she wasn't sure what she'd said. "Hi."

"Don't be silly. Your meeting with Marianne can wait." He glanced over at the editor. "Right?"

Marianne nodded. "Sure. Just give me a call when you're through." The editor disappeared down the long hallway, leaving Tenley standing alone in the door. Wasn't this how she'd imagined it? What was next?

"Come on in. Sit," he said, pointing to the chair on the other side of his desk. "God, you look…incredible."

"It's the new clothes," Tenley said. "Now that I'm an artist, I have to start dressing like one."

"They suit you," he said. "But then, everything looks good on you. I seem to remember a funny hat with earflaps. I liked that hat."

"I didn't bring it along. I didn't want to look like a complete bumpkin."

"So, are you really going back tonight? Because you can't. We have to have dinner. I'll take you out and show you the town." He reached for his phone and punched a button. "Carol, can you make a reservation for Tenley Marshall at the Drake? Confirm it for late arrival on our account."

Tenley shook her head. "I can't. I have to get back. I promised my grandfather."

"One of the suites would be good," he said to his secretary. When he hung up the phone, he nodded. "Just in case you don't want to go. You'll stay for dinner, right?"

"Sure. The traffic will probably be crazy until later on, anyway. So, yes, I'll stay for dinner."

"Good. We have a lot to catch up on. I can't believe you're here."

"I am," she said, slowly lowering herself into the chair. She set her portfolio on the floor, fumbling with the handles. Why had conversation suddenly become so difficult? She couldn't think of a single thing to say to him. He looked the same, maybe a bit more polished. He wore a finely tailored suit and a white dress shirt that showed off his dark features. If he'd picked out his clothes to please her, they were certainly doing the trick. He was as handsome as ever. "How have you been?"

"Good," he said. "You know, this is crazy. Good, fine, you look great." He circled around the desk, then stood in front of her, pulling her to her feet. Without hesitation, Alex cupped her face in his hands and gave her a gentle kiss. "That's better."

"I remember that," Tenley murmured, her gaze dropping to his lips.

"So do I." For a long time, they stood silently, staring at each other. And then, he blinked and glanced at his watch. "It's almost four. Let's go now and we'll have a few drinks before dinner and—"

"I have to see Marianne," she said, grabbing her portfolio.

"Right."

"But I won't be long. I'll come back at five and we'll go then."

"Sure," Alex said, following her to the door. "Her office is down there on the right. Name's on the door."

Tenley nodded and started down the hall. At the last minute, she glanced over her shoulder to find him watching her. "Stop staring at me," she said.

Alex laughed out loud and Tenley hurried down the hall, enjoying the sound. It hadn't gone badly. It could have been worse. They were able to be in the same room without jumping into each other's arms and tearing clothes off. And though the kiss was a bit more than what friends might share, they'd been a lot more than friends.

If this was all it was, Tenley could be happy. There was no anger or regret between them. Only good memories and a warm friendship. She could move on from there.

When she got to Marianne's office, she walked in, only to find another woman sitting in her guest chair. The woman jumped up and held out her hand. "Hello," she said. "I'm Tess Stamos. And you have got to be Tenley Marshall."

"Yes," she said.

"I'm Alex's sister. I work here, too. I loved your novel, by the way. It's about time women start kicking butt in those books, don't you think?"

"I do," Tenley said.

Tess was tall and slender, with dark hair and eyes. She appeared to be a few years older than Tenley, but she had a confidence that made her seem just a bit intimidating.

"So, you saw Alex? He's been going crazy all day waiting for you to come. He usually doesn't let a woman get him so rattled. You must be special."

"We're friends," Tenley said.

Tess observed her with a shrewd look. "I think you're more than that. Alex has even mentioned you to my mother, which means he's willing to put up with her nagging just so he can talk about you around the dinner table. But please, don't break my brother's heart or I will have to chop you into tiny pieces and run you through the printing press. I can do that, you know. I'm head of production."

With that, Tess Stamos waltzed out of the room, leaving Tenley with nothing to say except, "She was…nice."

Marianne circled her desk and took Tenley by the arm, guiding her toward a chair. "Don't let Tess bother you. She deals with loud printing presses and stubborn press operators all day long. She's used to speaking her mind."

As they went over the new drawings and story changes, Tenley's thoughts were occupied elsewhere. She'd expected a warm welcome, but there was something more going on. This wasn't just a casual visit, at least not for Alex. He'd been anticipating her arrival and had even told his sister about her. But then, as a new author, she would naturally be the subject of conversation around the office.

There was no need to read anything into Tess's words. Nothing had changed. Everybody was simply being kind and solicitous, just good business practice.

And at dinner tonight, she'd restrain herself, putting aside all the memories of their passionate encounters at her cabin. She was determined to make this relationship comfortable, to redraw the lines and follow the rules this time.

And though her heart ached a little bit for what they'd lost, Tenley could bear it. She was stronger now and able to look at the attraction between them with a practical eye. Though it would always be tempting, in the end, it just wasn't meant to be.

ALEX GUIDED THE SEDAN down Lakeshore Drive, impatient to get to the restaurant so that he could turn his full attention to the woman sitting beside him. It felt so good to have her back in his orbit again. Though they hadn't touched since he'd kissed her, just knowing he could reach out and make contact made him happy.

"How's your grandfather?" he asked.

"He's good. He says hello. He's working on a new series of paintings. Barns."

"And how are things in town? Is Randy giving you any problems?"

Tenley shook her head. "Actually, we're dating now. He just wore me down and I had to say yes. We're planning the wedding for June."

Alex frowned, then noticed the teasing smile twitching at the corners of her lips. "I'm very happy for you."

"What about you?" Tenley asked. "Have you been dating anyone?"

Alex was surprised by the question, but even more surprised by his answer. "Tenley, it's only been three weeks. I'm not interested in dating anyone."

"I just thought a charming guy like—"

He suddenly realized what she was getting at. "Oh, wait. I know where this is going. You looked me up on the Internet, didn't you? And you came up with that silly Web site."

"SmoothOperators.com. I didn't, Randy did. He gave me the full report."

"When?"

"Before you left. He dropped by the gallery when I was working."

"Damn, he doesn't give up, does he?"

"He's dating Linda Purnell now. So, yes, he has given

up. Unless he's carrying a secret torch for me." She glanced over at him. "Why haven't you started dating again?"

"Because I haven't met anyone half as interesting as you." In fact, Alex hadn't even bothered to go out since he got back to Chicago. He spent most of his evenings at the office, getting back to his apartment in time to catch the end of a basketball game or a hockey match. The rest of the night, he spent staring at his Black-Berry, trying to convince himself that not phoning Tenley was a good thing.

"I know what you mean. There aren't that many interesting single guys living in Sawyer Bay. Though prospects improve in the summer."

Alex reached out and grabbed her hand, lacing his fingers through hers. It felt so good to touch her. "We could skip the restaurant," he said. "We're just a couple blocks from the Drake. We could order room service and spend some time alone."

She smiled weakly and Alex immediately regretted his suggestion. He was moving too fast. And it was obvious her feelings for him had changed.

"I don't think that's a good idea," she said.

"You're probably right. Best to maintain a profes-sional relationship. But it worked out pretty well for us when we did it the first time."

"Yes, but that was just for fun."

Alex watched the traffic as it slowed in front of him for the light. What did she mean by that? Was that all he'd been to her, just a few nights of fun?

Maybe all this distance was simply her way of letting him down easy.

As they drove along the lakeshore, Alex pointed out the major landmarks. Acting as tour guide kept the conversation light and interesting. But in his head, he was cataloguing all the questions that needed answers. Why couldn't she love him? She didn't really believe that ridiculous Web site, did she?

They were so obviously compatible, both in and out of bed. He loved talking to her. She didn't babble like most of the women he'd dated. And she wasn't obsessed with her looks or her clothes. Over time, Alex had realized that it was the little things that he found so attractive.

Tenley didn't wear makeup, at least, not anymore. From the moment she got up in the morning until the time she went to bed, she never once looked in the mirror. She combed her hair with her fingers. She wore clothes that were comfortable and shoes that didn't kill her feet.

And she read books. She didn't watch silly television shows or buy fashion magazines. She had a stack of classics on her bedside table. She was smart and talented and witty.

"And when you have a free moment, you go out and do something useful with your time," he muttered, "rather than going to get your nails done."

"What?"

Alex glanced over to find Tenley watching him with an inquisitive expression. Had he said that out loud?

"Nothing," he said. "Here we are." Thankfully, the parking valet provided a distraction. He opened Tenley's door for her and helped her from the car, then circled around to grab the keys from Alex.

When they got inside, Tenley excused herself and headed toward the ladies' room. Alex waited outside and watched as two women went in and came out before Tenley. What was she doing in there? He reached for the door and pulled it open. "Tenley?"

"What?"

"Is everything all right?"

He heard a sniffle. "Yes?"

Alex stepped inside, then locked the door behind him. He heard the tears in her voice. She was locked in the center stall and he rapped on the door. "Come on, Tenley, open up. I don't want to have to crawl under."

He heard the latch flip and he pushed the door open. She sat on the toilet, her eyes red, a wad of toilet paper in her hand.

"Go away," she said.

"No." Alex reached down and took her hand, then pulled her out of the stall. "Why are you crying?"

"I don't know." This brought a fresh round of tears and she turned away from him and sat down on a small chair in the corner. "God, I hate crying. I feel so stupid."

"Are you upset with me?"

"No." She paused and wiped her nose. "Yes. Maybe. You just make it so difficult."

"What?" He pulled her into his arms and smoothed his hands along her waist. "I don't mean to."

Alex's fingers found her face and he tipped her gaze up to his. Her eyes were red and watery and he brushed a tear away with his thumb. He didn't have the words to make her feel better because he didn't know what was wrong. So Alex did the only thing he knew would take her mind off her troubles. He kissed her.

But what began as a sweet, soothing kiss, slowly turned into something more. Her mouth opened beneath his and he took what she offered. How many nights had he lain in bed, thinking about this, about the next time he'd touch her and kiss her and make love to her? This wasn't exactly the setting he'd imagined, but at this point, it didn't matter. Tenley was back in his arms again.

He grabbed the lapels of her jacket and pushed them aside, desperate to find a spot of bare skin to touch. They stumbled back against the sinks and Alex picked her up and set her on the edge of the counter, stepping between her legs.

She had too many clothes on and there wasn't enough time. He glanced over his shoulder and considered the stall for privacy, but decided against it. The door was locked. If someone knocked, they'd have to stop. But until then, he—

"No," she said, pressing her hands against his chest. "Don't do this."

Alex was stunned and he immediately stepped away. "What is it?"

She pulled her jacket back up and slid off the counter. "I can't do this. I—I have to go." Tenley hurried to the door and pulled on it, but it wouldn't open. "I need to go."

"Tenley, wait. I'm sorry. I didn't— It's just been such a long time and I—"

She finally realized the door was locked and when she turned the knob, it opened. He followed her out into the lobby, but she headed back out to the street.

"Tenley." He took her hand. "Where are you going?"

"I have to go home. I can't stay here."

"Don't. I promise, I won't kiss you again."

She raised her hand for a cab, but he pulled it down. A cab screeched to a halt in front of the restaurant. Christ, he could wait all day for a taxi and now, when he didn't want one, there were ten available. She pulled the door open.

"Wait," Alex said to the driver. "We're not through."

"Go," Tenley said.

"No! Wait." He reached into his pocket for his wallet, ready to pay the driver to do as ordered.

But Tenley pulled the door shut. "Go, now!" she shouted at the driver.

Alex could do nothing but curse as the taxi roared off down the street. The valet stood at his desk, observing the entire scene with a dubious expression.

"Bad date?" he asked.

"Yeah, you could say that."

"Well, at least you didn't buy her dinner." He grinned. "Do you want your car?"

Alex nodded. He sat down on a bench, his breath coming in gasps, clouding in front of his face in the cold air. What the hell had happened? Where was the woman who'd crawled into his bed and seduced him on the night they met? Or the woman who ran into the snow stark naked?

Something had happened to the free-spirited Tenley he knew three weeks ago. How could someone have changed so fast? He reached for his cell phone. She'd spent the previous night in a hotel and left her car parked there. Maybe if he tracked her down, he might catch her before she left.

Alex stared at his phone, then shook his head as he realized the impossibility of that task. The bottom line was Tenley didn't want to be with him. Whatever they'd shared had faded. And he'd just killed what was left of it with his behavior in the bathroom.

When the valet returned with his car, Alex gave him a fifty-dollar bill and slipped behind the wheel. He'd made only one mistake in his life and Alex suspected he'd never stop regretting it. He'd left Tenley that morning after his sister had called.

He should have stayed. He should have lived up there with her until he was absolutely certain she was in love with him. He knew her heart was fragile and yet he thought they'd just be able to pick up where they'd left off in a week or two. Only in the meantime, Tenley had erected a wall around herself, too high and too thick for him to broach.

He'd missed his chance with her and there was absolutely nothing he could do about it.

TENLEY LOOKED at her reflection in the mirror, trying to see herself as others might. Gone was the streak of purple in her hair. Gone was the dark eye makeup and the deep red lipstick, the black nail polish.

She smoothed her hands over the bodice of the red vintage dress. She'd found the garment in a trunk in her grandfather's attic and had thought the shawl collar and wide skirt made it a classic design. When she'd brought it down, her grandfather had grown all misty, remembering the night her grandmother had first worn it.

In her ongoing effort to get out more, Tenley had invited her grandfather to the Valentine's Dance, held at the fire hall in town. The dance was one of the biggest events of the winter season. Everyone attended. Jimmy Richter's Big Band came in from Green Bay to play and the Ladies Auxiliary made cake and pink punch. Anyone who was single was invited to attend, from teenagers to retirees.

Tenley suspected her grandfather had ulterior motives for accepting the date. Rumor had it he and Katie Vanderhoff had been seen together at Wednesday-night bingo for the past four weeks in a row. Though he might have wanted to ask Katie to the dance, Tenley knew the potential gossip would have scared him away. Considering the suitability of the match, the gossips would have had them married off before they stepped on the dance floor.

Tenley heard a knock on her door and she took one last look in the mirror. "You can do this," she murmured. "It's just a silly dance."

But it was more than that. Since her trip to Chicago, almost two weeks had passed. She'd begun to see her life in a different light. She wanted to find someone to love her, a man who might make her feel the way Alex did. But Tenley knew it would take time. She wouldn't fall in love in a week or even a year. There were too many things in her past that kept her from surrendering so easily.

But she had felt something with Alex and she was certain she could find that again if she only got out there and started looking. She had made one vow to herself. No more one-night stands. Sex for fun was a part of her past. From now on, she intended to act a bit more circumspect.

She grabbed her coat from the bed, then hurried to the door. The dogs tried to follow her outside, but she slipped out without them. "Sorry," she said.

Her grandfather stood on the porch, dressed in his best suit, his hands behind his back. He slowly brought out a plastic box and Tenley was delighted to find a corsage there. "It's an orchid," he said. "I used to buy your grandmother white orchids all the time. She loved them because they lasted so long."

Tenley took the box from his hand. "I'll put it on in the car. It'll freeze out here." She hurried down the steps and hopped inside her grandfather's Volvo. Shivering, she rubbed her hands together and then held them close to the heat. "Are you really sure you want to do this?" she asked.

"Your grandmother died four years ago. I think it's time I got out there and met some ladies. Not that I want to get married again, but I would like to have some company if I decide to see a movie or dine out."

He'd combed his bushy hair and shaved off the usual

stubble that covered his cheeks. "You look very hand-some," Tenley commented. "All the ladies will want to dance with you. I heard you've been spending time with Katie Vanderhoff."

He grinned. "Maybe. It's those damn cinnamon rolls. I stop by for coffee in the morning and she feeds me one of those and I think I'm in love. That's how your grandmother won my heart. With her apple pie."

"Well, you'll have to be sure to ask her to dance. Just make sure I get the first and the last one."

Tenley flipped the visor down and looked at her re-flection in the mirror. Her hair looked silly, all curled and poufed up. As soon as she got to the dance, she'd take it down.

"You look very pretty," her grandfather said, steering the car onto the road. "No more blue hair. Or was it purple? I can't remember."

"I've decided to be perfectly normal for one night. I'm even wearing underwear."

"I don't need to hear about that," her grandfather said, wagging his finger, "although, I am glad to hear it. I wouldn't want to have you twirling around on the dance floor wearing nothing beneath your skirt. And I do love to twirl a girl."

By the time they got to town, Tenley was nervous. She'd been off the social radar for so long she knew her appearance would cause a lot of speculation. Ev-eryone in town knew about Alex and her romance with him. But as far as they understood, that was still going on, long distance.

If they asked, she would have to tell them the truth—she and Alex had parted as friends. Friends who didn't speak to each other. Friends who couldn't possibly be in the same room without wanting to tear each other's clothes off.

The dance was already well under way when they arrived. Her grandfather grabbed her coat and hung it up, then held out his arm gallantly, a broad smile on his face. "You look lovely. Absolutely lovely. I wish your grandmother could see you. You look just as pretty as she did on the night we met."

"Thank you," Tenley said. "Are you ready?"

"I am. Are you?"

She nodded. They walked toward the entrance to the hall and stopped at the ticket table. Harvey Willis's sister, Ellen, was selling tickets and complimented them both on their snazzy attire.

The interior of the firehouse had been transformed. The trucks had been moved outside for the night and lights had been strung from the overhead beams. A small stage was set up on one end and the band was already in the midst of their rendition of "Moon River."

To Tenley's relief, there were plenty of familiar faces in attendance. If no one asked her to dance, she'd at least be able to chat. But as she scanned the room, her gaze came to rest on a face she hadn't expected to see.

Her fingers dug into her grandfather's arm as she gasped. "He's here," she whispered.

"Who's here?"

"Alex. He's standing right over there."

"Oh, look at that," her grandfather said. "Now, doesn't he look handsome. And what's that he has in his arms? Looks like roses."

"Did you know about this?" Tenley asked.

"Well, he did call a few days ago. Wanted to know if the dance was on Saturday or Sunday night. I just told him what he wanted to know. I also mentioned you'd be attending." He unhooked Tenley's hand from his arm and gave her a little push. "Go on. Talk to him before some other girl snaps him up."

Tenley slowly crossed the hall. Everyone was watching, even some of the guys in the band. Her knees felt weak and her head was spinning, but she held her emotions in check. She was not going to break down and cry. Nor was she going to throw herself into his arms.

She stopped in front of him, swallowing hard before speaking. "What are you doing here?"

"I heard you were planning on attending and I didn't want to give any of these single guys a chance to charm you."

"How did you know about the dance?"

"You mentioned it. You said Randy asked you every year."

"You remember that?"

He nodded. "I remember everything you said to me."

She glanced over her shoulder at her grandfather and found him grinning from ear to ear.

"I brought you something," Alex said. He handed her the roses. "I'm sorry there's so many of them, but I asked for the nicest bouquet and this is what they gave me." He took them from her arms. "Here, we'll just put them down."

"Thank you," she said.

"And there's candy and a card, but I thought I'd save that until later. They're out in the car."

"Gee, all you forgot was the jewelry," she teased.

"Ah, no. I didn't forget that." Alex reached into his pants pocket, but when he didn't find what he was looking for, he patted down his jacket pockets. "Where did I put that?"

"I don't need any more gifts, Alex. The flowers are fine."

"No, you'll like this one," he said. "At least, I hope you will. Here it is." He held out his fist, then opened it.

Lying in his palm was a ring…a diamond ring…a very large diamond ring. Tenley gasped, her gaze fixed on it. It was the most beautiful thing she'd ever seen, a pale yellow heart-shaped diamond, surrounded by tiny white diamonds.

"What does that mean?" she asked. Was this a proposal? And if it was, did he really expect her to accept with all these people watching her? Or maybe that was why he'd done it here, so she couldn't refuse. "Alex, I don't think this is a good idea. You know how I—"

"Tenley, don't talk, just listen. Yes, I know how you feel. And I understand your hesitation. Your experiences in life haven't made it easy for you to open yourself up to loving someone. But what we shared that week in your cabin was something special and I don't want to let that go."

"Is this a proposal?"

"It's whatever you want it to be," Alex said. "You decide. All I know is I don't want to lose you. I want you to be mine, for now and for as long as you'll have me. I want you to be my valentine, Tenley."

"But I—"

"Don't say no. You can't say no. Because I'm going to keep coming back every weekend and every holiday until you say yes. I'll buy a place up here and I'll come over every morning and take you to breakfast. And I'll sit on your sofa every night and rub your feet. We'll go for walks in the woods in the winter and we'll take our clothes off and lie in the summer sun."

He took her hand and slipped the ring on her finger. "I'm giving this to you so that you understand I won't change my mind. For as long as you wear that ring, I'm completely yours."

"But how are we going to do this? You live in Chicago and I live here."

"I'm not sure. At first, I'll come up on the weekends. And maybe you can come down and visit. We'll figure out all the details later, Tenley. We don't have to decide everything right now. All we have to do is make a commitment to try."

He was making it so easy for her to say yes. And she wanted to say the word, to throw herself into his arms and tell him it was quite possible that she did love him. Not just possible, very probable.

"I was thinking about spending some time in Chicago. There are some classes I want to take at the Art Institute this summer."

He smiled. "Really? Because that's just a quick train ride from where I live. You could stay with me. I could take you out and show you the city. You could even bring the dogs and cats. I've got plenty of room for all of you." He dropped down on one knee and held her hand. "Say yes, Tenley. Tell me you're willing to try."

"Yes." The word came out of her mouth without a second thought. "Yes. I am willing to try. And I will be your valentine."

Alex stood up and pulled her into his arms, lifting her off her feet and twirling her around on the dance floor. The crowd around them erupted in wild applause and Tenley looked up to find everyone in the hall watching them. A warm blush flooded her cheeks and she buried her face in the curve of Alex's neck.

"We're causing a scene," he said.

"I know. Don't worry. It will give them something to gossip about tomorrow morning."

"Are you all right with that?"

She nodded. "I think I can handle it."

Alex set her back on her feet, then took her face in his hands and kissed her. That brought even more applause and a few moments later, the band broke into their rendition of "My Funny Valentine." Alex swept her out onto the dance floor.

She'd never really danced before, but Alex seemed to know exactly what he was doing. She followed his lead and before long, they looked like experts. Everything always seemed so much easier when he was around.

Life, love—and dancing.

Epilogue

ANGELA TACKED an index card on her bulletin board. "The Charmer," she said. "I've discovered ten archetypes of the typical male seducer. Once women learn to identify each type, then they'll be prepared to judge their relationships more objectively."

"So, who are you planning to interview for this chapter?" Ceci asked.

"I wanted to interview Alex Stamos. He seemed to fit the type perfectly. But when I called him last week, his sister told me that he's been involved with a woman for nearly two months. That doesn't fit the pattern."

"Do you think he could be in love?" Ceci asked.

"No," Angela said. She paused. "Well, maybe. But that would be an aberration. The majority of these men never change."

"Yeah, but we'd like to believe they could," Ceci said.

"Well, I'll just have to find another man to interview. The Charmer is the most common of the archetypes. It shouldn't be too difficult."

Angie sat down at her desk and picked up the description she'd been working on. "The Charmer is all talk. He knows exactly what to say to get what he wants and he enjoys wielding this power over women. He will often delay a physical relationship, waiting until it's your idea to hop into bed together. While you're certain that sex will take the relationship to a more intimate level, he knows it signals the end. He quickly moves on after blaming you for getting too serious, too fast."

"Sounds good," Ceci said. "But it would be nice to believe that, given the right woman, any guy could change his bad behavior." She sighed. "Kind of makes me wonder what happened to all those guys I dumped because I thought they were hopeless causes."

In truth, Angela had been wondering the same thing. Was she wrong about these men? Could you teach an old dog new tricks? Or were some of these men just lost causes? "I suppose we have to be optimistic," she murmured. "If not, we might as well just give up now, because the bad ones far outnumber the good ones."

"I guess I'd really like to know how much time you should give a guy before you cut your losses and move on," Ceci said. "I've been with Lance for three months and he still refuses to call me his girlfriend."

Angela gave her friend a weak smile. "There are always exceptions to every rule. We've just got to figure out a way to find those exceptions."

Angela stared at the index card. Alex's change of heart certainly didn't bode well for the theories she planned to present in her book. But for every one guy who left the single life behind and fell in love, there were a hundred more serial daters out there breaking women's hearts.

She was on a mission to make a point. And if Alex Stamos wasn't the man she thought he was, then she'd find another Charmer to take his place. After all, she could spot a smooth operator a mile away.

* * * * *

*Rancher Ramsey Westmoreland's temporary cook
is way too attractive for his liking.
Little does he know Chloe Burton came to his ranch
with another agenda entirely....*

That man across the street had to be, without a doubt, the most handsome man she'd ever seen.

Chloe Burton's pulse beat rhythmically as he stopped to talk to another man in front of a feed store. He was tall, dark and every inch of sexy—from his Stetson to the well-worn leather boots on his feet. And from the way his jeans and Western shirt fit his broad muscular shoulders, it was quite obvious he had everything it took to separate the men from the boys. The combination was enough to corrupt any woman's mind and had her weakening even from a distance. Her body felt flushed. It was hot. Unsettled.

Over the past year the only male who had gotten her time and attention had been the e-mail. That was simply pathetic, especially since now she was practically drooling simply at the sight of a man. Even his stance— both hands in his jeans pockets, legs braced apart, was a pose she would carry to her dreams.

And he was smiling, evidently enjoying the conversation being exchanged. He had dimples, incredibly sexy dimples in not one but both cheeks.

"What are you staring at, Clo?"

Chloe nearly jumped. She'd forgotten she had a

lunch date. She glanced over the table at her best friend from college, Lucia Conyers.

"Take a look at that man across the street in the blue shirt, Lucia. Will he not be perfect for Denver's first issue of *Simply Irresistible* or what?" Chloe asked with so much excitement she almost couldn't stand it.

She was the owner of *Simply Irresistible,* a magazine for today's up-and-coming woman. Their once-a-year Irresistible Man cover, which highlighted a man the magazine felt deserved the honor, had increased sales enough for Chloe to open a Denver office.

When Lucia didn't say anything but kept staring, Chloe's smile widened. "Well?"

Lucia glanced across the booth at her. "Since you asked, I'll tell you what I see. One of the Westmorelands—Ramsey Westmoreland. And, yes, he'd be perfect for the cover, but he won't do it."

Chloe raised a brow. "He'd get paid for his services, of course."

Lucia laughed and shook her head. "Getting paid won't be the issue, Clo—Ramsey is one of the wealthiest sheep ranchers in this part of Colorado. But everyone knows what a private person he is. Trust me—he won't do it."

Chloe couldn't help but smile. The man was the epitome of what she was looking for in a magazine cover and she was determined that whatever it took, he would be it.

"Umm, I don't like that look on your face, Chloe. I've seen it before and know exactly what it means."

She watched as Ramsey Westmoreland entered the

store with a swagger that made her almost breathless.
She *would* be seeing him again.

* * * * *

Look for Silhouette Desire's
HOT WESTMORELAND NIGHTS
by Brenda Jackson,
available March 9 wherever books are sold.

THE WESTMORELANDS

NEW YORK TIMES
bestselling author

BRENDA JACKSON

HOT WESTMORELAND NIGHTS

Ramsey Westmoreland knew better than to lust
after the hired help. But Chloe, the new cook,
was just so delectable. Though their affair was
growing steamier, Chloe's motives became
suspicious. And when he learned Chloe was
carrying his child this Westmoreland Rancher
had to choose between pride or duty.

Available March 2010 wherever books are sold.

Always Powerful, Passionate and Provocative.

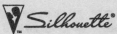

REQUEST YOUR FREE BOOKS!

2 FREE NOVELS
PLUS 2
FREE GIFTS!

HARLEQUIN®

Blaze

Red-hot reads!

HBIO

COMING NEXT MONTH

Available February 23, 2010

www.eHarlequin.com